THE AUTHOR

Billy Bob Buttons is a young talented author. On top of being a secondary school English teacher, he is also a pilot.

Born in the Viking city of York, he and his wife, Therese, a true Swedish girl from the IKEA county of Småland, now live in Stockholm and London. Their twin girls, Rebecca and Beatrix, and little boy, Albert, inspire Billy Bob every day to pick up a pen and work on his books.

When not writing, he enjoys tennis and playing 'MONSTER!' with his three children.

He is the author of the much loved, The Gullfoss Legends, Rubery Award finalist, Felicity Brady and the Wizard's Bookshop, UK People's Book Prize runner-up, TOR Assassin Hunter and TOR Wolf Rising.

I Think I Murdered Miss, his ninth children's novel, won the UK People's Book Prize in 2014.

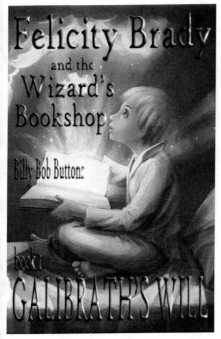

Felicity Brady and the Wizard's Bookshop

Billy Bob Buttons

book 1
GALIBRATH'S WILL

Felicity Brady and the Wizard's Bookshop

Billy Bob Buttons

book 2
ARTICULUS QUEST

Felicity Brady and the Wizard's Bookshop

Billy Bob Buttons

book 3
INCANTUS GOTHMOG

by award-winning author
Billy Bob Buttons

The gripping story
of a magical legend

the
GULLFOSS
legends

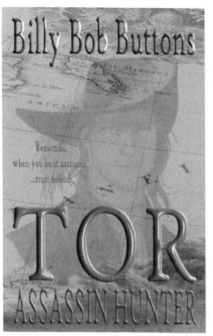

Billy Bob Buttons

Remember, when you hunt assassins ...trust nobody.

TOR
ASSASSIN HUNTER

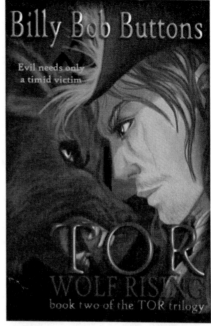

Billy Bob Buttons

Evil needs only a timid victim

TOR
WOLF RISING
book two of the TOR trilogy

I THINK I
MURDERED MISS

BUS
STOP

BY THE AWARD-WINNING
BILLY BOB BUTTONS

'Muffins and a big, hungry   ...the perfect children's book recipe.'
Kids' Zone

FROM THE
AWARD-WINNING,
BEST-SELLING

Muffin
MONSTER

CHILDREN'S NOVELS BY BILLY BOB BUTTONS

FELICITY BRADY AND THE WIZARD'S BOOKSHOP

GALIBRATH'S WILL
ARTICULUS QUEST
INCANTUS GOTHMOG
GLUMWEEDY'S DEVIL
CROWL'S CREEPERS

THE GULLFOSS LEGENDS

TOR
ASSASSIN HUNTER

TOR
WOLF RISING

I THINK I MURDERED MISS

MUFFIN MONSTER

COMING SOON

TOR
MUTINY'S CLAW

TIFFANY SPARROW
SPOOK SLAYER

THE WISHING SHELF PRESS

Published by THE WISHING SHELF PRESS, UK.
ISBN 978 0 9574767 4 5
www.felicitybrady.co.uk www.bbbuttons.co.uk
Printed and bound by BOOK PRINTING UK.
Edited by Alison Emery, Therese Råsbäck and Svante
Jurnell.
Cover by www.redwombatstudio.com

Felicity Brady

and the Wizard's Bookshop

Billy Bob Buttons

book 4

GLUMWEEDY'S DEVIL

For my sister, Jane, and my cousins, Peter and Bernard, who never got to curl up on a sofa and enjoy a good book.

Chapter 1

Johnny Depp of the Wizard World

"Ow! My foot!"

"Oy! Fatty! Y' mamma is so fat when she wears yellow, people shout, 'TAXI!'"

Shrugging off the angry yells, Fester Glumweedy, the new mayor of Twice Brewed, bulldozed his way down the wigglefinch-poo splattered steps just next to the town's old bridge.

He was in a lip-smackingly good mood. He had just nipped into The Droopy Wand Café for a dish of sugar-frosted spiders, a bowl of piping hot dragon-tongue soup and a bag of grilled goblin fingers.

On top of this, he had that very morning managed to stuff a dorfmoron and a tiny wizard full of straw.

The dorfmoron had been a warlord called Jumble Mud who had been stabbed in the chest during the recent battle for Lupercus Castle, and the wizard, in his green sparkly boots, the malevolent Incantus Gothmog.

Admittedly, even for a master taxidermist like Glumweedy, they had been challenging jobs. After accidentally popping the dorfmoron's googly eyes, he had been forced to stuff old golf balls in the sockets. Not very tidy. Then he had run out of straw with a floppy leg and two deflated hands still to go. The barrel-shaped wizard chuckled. A bowl of mushed-up yukocot had sorted that, no problem.

Anyway, the loopy hook-nosed professor at the Twice Brewed Museum of Stuffed

Monsters and Evil P E Teachers, had been as happy as a glow worm on Guy Fawkes night.

"I shall stick Jumble Mud in the front window," he had announced, flapping his arms in a very un-professor-like way, "next to that skinny Gothmog-fellow. Oh, and can you stuff a goblin for me? Nasty bit of work called Bartholomew Banks." Glumweedy remembered he had then sniffed his hands. "Can you smell yukocot?"

At the bottom of the steps, Glumweedy stopped, his piggy eyes wandering over to a door partly hidden in the shadow of the bridge. Grunting, he grabbed for a gold watch hanging from his velvet jacket and glared at it. Where was Ratchet!? They had planned to meet almost an hour ago. To Glumweedy, it was very important to turn up to every meeting last. It helped him to feel important and Glumweedy liked wizards to think he was important. But it looked as if the chap from The Planning Office was going to be even later.

Blast him!

He ambled over to a rickety-looking fence and glared down at the River Cruor. The water rushed by, carrying lumps of jagged ice and clumps of trees. Over the last week or so, the sun had been braving the sky, sending the clouds scurrying away in horror and melting the snow. Glumweedy always preferred the summer. Soon it would be goblin shooting season and his 'Stuff Y' Pets' shop would be crammed full of customers.

Whipping out a silk hanky, he lifted up his bowler hat and wiped his clammy brow and bald head. He turned around, looking back at the flaking door and the jumble of old books crammed up to the window of the bookshop. He smirked. Soon, he'd own a second, bigger shop. This shop.

A witch wrapped up in a dirty grey shawl tottered by. Glumweedy winked at her, quickly plopping his hat back on to hide the bald patch. "Do you mind if I stare at you," he crooned, "so I can remember you in my dreams."

The witch rolled her eyes and snorted. Picking up her feet, she scrambled up the steps to the High Street. "Sleaze ball," she muttered.

Fester pretended not to catch her cruel words and congratulated himself on how charming he had been. In his eyes, he was a bit of a catch, the 'Johnny Depp' of the wizard world. But in fact, he looked like the 'Nutty Professor'. He was very fat and had a bum that drooped down to the backs of his knees. His feet were frying-pan shaped and he always seemed to have a rash on his legs where the flab rubbed. Piggy eyes and a tiny skewiff nose made his face look almost vacant as if they had shrivelled up or run away in disgust, and his lips and the top half of his chin hid under a bushy walrus moustache.

He had on a black jacket and trousers, his boots buffed to mirrors.

"Mayor Glumweedy! Mayor Glumweedy!" A lanky man, his twig legs as spindly as the umbrella clutched in his hand, was hurrying down the steps. He had a brown satchel slung over his shoulder.

The fat wizard tapped the face of his gold watch. "Hurry up," he grumbled. "The Droopy Wand Café shuts soon." Reluctantly, he shook the man's hand. He hated touching skin, unless it was dead and needed stuffing.

Bypassing red and turning maroon, the man looked as if his hand had just been trapped in a jar of sweets. "Sorry, Mayor," he mumbled. "I had to go to a sewer meeting. Bloodgrub rats. Big teeth. Four eyes. A devil to kill."

Glumweedy's lips twisted into a sneer. "Thrilling stuff," he scoffed.

"My boss was there so I had to stay till the end. Numbskull, talk for Eternus, blah, blah, blah..." He continued to mumble his apology as he rummaged in his satchel and yanked out a stack of crumpled papers.

"You got my letter, Ratchet?" Glumweedy interrupted him.

"Oh, yes, Mayor. An imp dropped it off on Thursday." He hooked a monocle over his left eye and squinted at the top sheet. "I see from your form here that you wish to open a second 'Stuff Y' Pets' shop." He cast a troubled glance at the wizard. "Is that correct?"

Glumweedy nodded eagerly, grinding his teeth. Snapping his fingers, a scroll of parchment jumped out of his jacket pocket. He unrolled it, balancing it on the top of the fence. "If you have a gander at this," he commanded Ratchet. "I want to put a new swivel door here, thatch the roof and fill in the chimney. Next I want to get rid of the steps, brick up the window and knock down a wall here, here and here. Oh, and squeeze a carpet park over there so this old fence will have to go too."

Glancing down at the drawings, Ratchet rubbed his crooked nose. He had broken it in a football match he had been refereeing. A Twice Brewed F. C. fan had smacked him in the chops when his team had lost 101-0 to Cauldron City Wanderers. He had given twenty-seven free kicks and thirty-two corners in that match, all to Cauldron City.

In return, the City players had presented him with a silver watch. Silver plated, anyway, he had discovered when he had later pawned it.

"To do all this, you will have to bulldoze half of the shop. You do understand that this is The Wishing Shelf? Magic books have been sold in there for over a thousand years."

"It must be this shop," snapped Glumweedy. "Remember, The Wishing Shelf is not just a bookshop, it is the doorway to hundreds of lands. Just think of it, all them wizards travelling here, there and everywhere and all of them going through Stuff Y' Pets. I will be swimming in gold."

Looking rather sceptical, Ratchet nodded. "Anyway, the shop's now owned by a fellow called, let me see, Tantalus Falafel I think..."

"He's dead," butted in Glumweedy. "Six feet under. Croaked. Popped off. Hopped the lily pad. Pity, he was a good customer. Big hunter, you see. He was killed in that battle over by Lupercus Castle. Stabbed by Jumble Mud, so I was told."

Scowling, Ratchet scribbled on his hand. "Tantalus Falafel, two f's, two l's, yes?"

Glumweedy shrugged, looking bored.

"My office was not informed," Ratchet grumbled. "Really, if wizards do insist on getting killed they should try and let us know.

Anyway, he must have left the shop to his son or daughter..."

"No, no son, no kids at all, so under the new law, no problem." Glumweedy grinned wickedly, grinding his teeth even louder. He always did this when he got excited. "Not if I get lots of wizards and hags to sign my scroll," he added shrewdly.

Ratchet nodded, his eyes glued to the paper bag of goblin fingers in Glumweedy's hand. "So, what you got in there?"

"Oh, er, moth balls," fibbed the wizard. He never shared his food.

"Oh, okay, but I must slip this letter in The Wishing Shelf." He looked slyly at Glumweedy. "The new owner needs to know what's going on too." Pulling a yellow scroll from his satchel, he turned to the door. "It is only right," he finished stubbornly.

"Hey! Hey! Relax." Grabbing him by the shoulder, Glumweedy shot him a meaningful stare. "I can do that. An important wizard from The Planning Office posting letters! Why, it's below you. And the shop's so far out of your way."

Ratchet frowned and put on a show of looking confused. He even scratched his brow. "But the door's just over there," he blustered back.

"Hey?" All of a sudden Glumweedy seemed to be deaf. "For you," he declared, stuffing a red envelope in his hand. "Two tickets to the ballet. Dragon Puddle is on. A VIW box for you and your pretty wife."

Tasting his lips, Ratchet snatched for the tickets, stuffing them in his pocket. His mind popped back two weeks to when he had finally got his sticky paws on the landlady of Ye Olde Banshee pub, in the broom closet next to the beer cellar. He had only popped in for a bag of nuts!

His 'not so pretty' wife would be staying in to do the dusting.

"And, by the way, is this your very big bag of emeralds?" He yanked a bulging canvas sack out of his trouser pocket and showed it to the drooling wizard. "I found it on the top step, just under the lamp. Almost tripped over it. Wink! Wink!"

The thinner man's eyes bulged greedily, the scowl seeming to jump off his face. "Yes, yes," he blurted out, grabbing for the neck of the bag. "On the steps, you say? How clumsy of me to drop it." Sweating profusely, he slipped it hastily under his robe.

Glancing fretfully over his shoulder, he stuffed the scroll in Glumweedy's hand. "Must be off," he prattled. "Ye Olde Banshee pub is calling. But pop in and see me. You know where my office is."

The other wizard smirked, fingering the scroll's ribbon. "I will see you shortly," he shouted to Ratchet's receding back, "so you can sign The Wishing Shelf over to me."

He watched the scrawny wizard scramble back up the steps to the High Street.

"Wimp," he muttered. Ratchet was too easily bribed and not to be trusted, which was why he had not told him all of his plans for The Wishing Shelf.

Another hag marched by. Glumweedy tipped his hat, stretching his lips and baring his crooked teeth. "Do you have a map," he slimed, "because I keep getting lost in your eyes."

The hag gagged, conjured up a bag and pretended to be sick in it. "Hippo hips," she choked.

Shrugging, Glumweedy ballooned his cheeks. "There's no fat on me," he muttered. "I'm just fluffy."

Spinning on his heel, he draped his elbows on the top of the old, crooked fence. It sagged under him, whining like a mule.

He watched a wigglefinch bobbing up and down on the river. If only he had a rock, he pondered. They were a doddle to stuff.

Popping his lips, Glumweedy scrunched up the scroll and tossed it at the chirruping bird. Squawking, it flew away, pooping on the wizard's left shoulder. Glumweedy gritted his teeth. Then, he dug his hand in the paper bag, grabbed hold of a goblin finger and stuffed it in his jaws.

Chapter 2

Doctor Besaggy's Herd of Sheep

Twiddling her thumbs, Felicity lay stretched out on top of her bed. She had on yellow pyjamas covered in tiny dinosaurs; a Stegosaurus lay slumped on her pocket and a Tyrannosaurus growled in her armpit.

A pretty girl, or so her mum told her, she had long wavy locks to her shoulders and her cheeks were all freckly (fifty-two freckles in fact. Lucy had counted them in cookery class). Felicity always looked a little pale as if she lived in a cellar. That, or she had a spot of vampire blood in her and the sun scared her and kept her indoors. She always had on jeans and old jumpers and her front tooth had a crack in it after her baby brother, Samuel, had

had a tantrum and had thrown a bowl of corn flakes at her.

She looked over to her dad. He was hunched up on a stool by the window, gazing out at the black clouds hanging over the hospital. She was happy he was there, to comfort her, to tell her to eat up all her sprouts and to turn off the telly and open her maths book, but he did look as if he had not slept in a week. His eyes were dull and every second or so, he scratched his bristly chin.

Her mum was perched on the end of the bed reading Hello magazine. Every so often, she informed her husband of George Clooney's latest film and who he was dating. As Felicity watched her, she saw her suck in her cheeks in annoyance. She wondered what Mr Clooney had done to annoy her.

"Where is that Doctor Besaggy?" she snapped, dropping the magazine by her feet.

"He'll be along soon," Felicity soothed her. Her mum looked tired too. She had a fresh wrinkle underlining her left eye and she had forgotten to put on lipstick. "I guess he has lots of sick people to see."

Her dad winked at her and mustered a grin. He thought she was being brave but, in fact, she hated seeing Doctor Besaggy. Every day on his rounds he stopped by to tell her to, 'Try to relax, try to sleep, try not to worry.' Now, when he stood by her bed, glaring at her chart and tutting, she just wanted to dig her nose in the pillow and duck under the sheets.

Felicity's eyes found the small table next to her bed. She wrinkled up her nose. On it was her maths book and a tray of food. The nurse had told her it was chicken hotpot but it looked like mashed up Pedigree Chum to her. She had begun to number her food, best bits first. Carrots usually got a three, cauliflower a two – she liked cauliflower – and sprouts, the biggest number she could think of. Then, she'd eat the nasty stuff first and the yummy stuff she saved till last. This was now the highlight of her day.

"So, how long did the doctor say?" her mum blurted out.

Felicity swallowed. It was as if a walnut was stuck in her throat. "Six weeks, at best." This is how long Doctor Besaggy had told her it would be until she was up on her feet. "But I will need to do lots of stretching."

"Stretching," echoed Mr Brady. "Good." He nodded enthusiastically. He understood stretching. He was in the army. "Work hard, my girl. Show him you can do it in only three weeks. Try doing a few push-ups too."

"It is not a race," his wife scolded him.

Mr Brady shrugged. "No, no, of course not." But he snuck Felicity a wink anyway.

Hickory Crowl and Kitta had told her parents over a week ago that she had broken her legs and so far, they had been brilliant. They had not even quizzed her on how it had happened. It seemed the wizard had told them she'd fallen down the steps next to The Wishing Shelf and they had been happy to nod and agree on how slippery they were.

"I shall be telephoning the council," her dad had declared.

So the fact that Incantus Gothmog had crushed her legs under a shelf of deviant books had, so far, not come up.

"Your brother is missing you. Aunty Imelda told me on the phone."

Felicity smiled at her mum. "I miss his tiny fingers. When is he back?"

Samuel was staying with his aunty in Ferwig for two weeks, giving Mr and Mrs Brady time to visit Felicity in hospital every day. He was probably enjoying a diet of Kit-Kats and hot cocoa and being dressed in trendy new tops and tiny sandals from M&S. Aunty Imelda was very chic.

Lucky kid!

Just then, Doctor Besaggy strolled up the ward. He reminded Felicity of a king who felt he had to visit the poor every now and then. A very odd-looking chap, his top lip often twitched and crow's feet snaked off his eyes. He had the beefy shoulders of a bricklayer and the skinny legs of a kitchen stool. Felicity often wondered why he did not just topple over. Her mum whipped a lipstick out of her bag. Felicity had a feeling she had fallen in love.

Her dad rolled his eyes.

Besaggy swaggered over to her bed, a herd of young doctors crowded on his heels like a flock sheep.

"So, my little strawberry, how do we feel today?"

Did he say 'We'? *She* had the metal rods in her legs. And why did he keep calling her a strawberry? But the word, "Okay," popped out, followed by, "But my feet keep getting cold."

Besaggy's eyes twinkled. "Hmm." He rubbed his chin. "A touch of footynitus, I think."

The sheep seemed to find this terrible joke very funny and fell about laughing, but Felicity just gritted her teeth and felt sorry for his poor wife. Her mum giggled so she turned to glare at her. She spotted she had now slapped on green sparkly eyeshadow too.

Looking smug, Besaggy snatched up the chart off the end of her bed. "Soon be time for you to begin therapy," he announced, studying it. "Don't worry, we'll go easy at first. But I want you out of that bed. You'll be getting welts on your bottom. Start tomorrow, first thing." He put a tick on her chart.

Felicity stiffened. This is what she had been most hoping for, but now it was here, she was scared. "You really think so? They still hurt a lot. I feel as if I was thrown off a skyscraper. Maybe..."

"Now, now, strawberry," he admonished her, "why put it off?" He winked at her, popped the chart back on the hook, and moved off to find his next victim. His herd of sheep followed meekly at his heels.

"Excellent news." Her dad ruffled her curls and grinned at her.

Felicity nodded and worked on trying not to look too bummed, but her lips seemed to have forgotten how to smile. She decided to change the subject. "So, when do we head off to Catterick?"

Mr and Mrs Brady exchanged a look. "Probably not going to go now," admitted her dad at last. "This hospital is very good and we want you to stay here till you feel better. For the best, we think."

"But your new job?"

Mr Brady shrugged. "Seeing you up and walking is what's important to me, not how many arrows I have on my shoulders."

Felicity nodded slowly. She knew she should be really happy. This is what she had wanted; to stay in Twice Brewed and work in The Wishing Shelf. But why had Kitta and Hickory not visited her? She did not even know if they had defeated Incantus Gothmog's army. She remembered what the doctor had told her, how bad the scarring on her legs would be. She felt tears welling up in her eyes. Right now, the magic bookshop was the last place in the world, any world, she wanted to be.

"Darling?"

Felicity looked at her mum.

"I'm going to pop a beef-and-pickle roll in your drawer here," she dug in her shopping bag, "and a packet of HobNobs." She glanced at the tray of food and scowled. "Got to keep your energy up."

Her dad leant over and kissed her brow. "See you tomorrow, luv."

Felicity mustered a tiny smile. "See you soon." She watched as they walked away, her mum stopping for a second to chat to a nurse.

Probably to have a grumble about the chicken hotpot.

Every bed in her ward was full, but Felicity liked hardly any of them. A girl, a bit older than her, had broken her legs too. But she seemed to enjoy telling the doctors how fast she had been driving when she had hit the wall. There was a thin woman, two beds down, who had lung cancer and kept popping out for a 'fag', and the chap in the next bed was so fat, a nurse had discovered mould in his armpits. Even now, she could tell he was eyeing up her HobNobs. The only person Felicity felt sorry for was a lady in the very end bed, who was so polite she even thanked the doctors when they stuck a needle in her bum cheek.

Felicity's eyes snapped open. Quickly, she jumped up in bed, but instantly regretted it as her legs shouted at her in protest. Rubbing her aching knee, she glanced around the dimly lit ward. Everybody seemed to be fast asleep, the plump chap in the next bed snoring like a baby elephant. Perhaps it had been him who had woken her?

Suddenly there was a flash of green light and the window next to her bed sprung open. Felicity gulped and pulled her sheets up to her chin. A moment later, a blond man popped his head in and grinned at her. "Looking for a girl called Felicity. She's got murky, brown eyes, glowing red cheeks and a sparkling smile."

"Hickory!?" Did he just say 'murky'?

The wizard hopped in the open window and tiptoed over to her bed. He kissed her on the cheek. Felicity, who had a mad crush on Hickory, felt her face glow red.

"Wotcha," he whispered, sitting on the edge of her bed. "How do you feel?"

A battle raged in her head. She had been very upset he had not yet been to see her. But should she be stroppy or not? "Not too bad," she allowed. She'd be stroppy later and the kiss had helped.

"Wonderful! And the legs? Soon be on your feet doing the tango, yes?"

Felicity grimaced and looked down the bed. She had on her pyjamas but only her bare feet were sticking out of the bottom of the sheet. "Doctor Besaggy reckons another six weeks."

Hickory's jaw dropped open in disgust. "You gotta be kidding." He glanced over his shoulder. "Here, pop this on your foot."

Felicity's eyes sprung open. "Pardon?"

She watched in horror as the wizard slipped a brass ring on her big toe. If only it had been her wedding finger, she thought wistfully. Hanging from it was what looked like a bloody lump of fur.

"Bit of a 'pick me up'. A gift from Dorothy. Remember her?" Dorothy was a witch who had helped Hickory when he had been badly burnt.

She nodded. "What is it?" She glared at her foot as if it had just kicked her in the face.

"A shubablybub finger."

Felicity grimaced. So, it was a bloody lump of fur, although she had no idea what a shubablybub was. However, she did have a sneaky feeling Doctor Besaggy was not going to be very pleased.

"How will it help?" She was a bit scared to ask.

"Not a clue. But it smells a bit of muddy dog." He winked cheekily at her.

Felicity's tummy twisted in a tight knot. To her he was the best looking man in the world, apart from Brad Pitt and the chap who played Indiana Jones, but he was getting a bit old now. Sadly, Hickory had lost his hand. The wizard had been a crook and a goblin had chiselled it off when he had got nabbed trying to nick a goblet. No matter. She adored him anyway.

"Here." He handed her a small red book. Her diary!

She blushed and took it.

"Kitta stumbled on it. That and a mushy yukocot. I dumped the yukocot, by the way."

She nodded briskly and slipped it under her pillow, praying the wizard had not looked in it.

Hickory squeezed her shoulder. "Sorry I took so long coming to see you. Been busy helping in the hospital, you see. A lot were injured in the battle. That's where I bumped into Dorothy."

"Hospital?" Felicity glanced around the ward.

"No, no, no." He patted her head. "In Eternus, not in England. Hey, guess what?"

"What?"

"Guess."

"You bought me a bunch of grapes?"

"Nope. Should I have? Sorry. But I do have a surprise for you."

Felicity hoped it was a second kiss.

Abruptly, the wizard spun on his heel and dashed off. But he was soon back, pushing a wheelchair. "In you get." Gently, he helped her in and then pushed her over to the window.

"What am I looking for?" All she could see was the moon and the silhouette of a garden.

"Over there. Under the willow tree."

"What willow – AH HA!!" Suddenly the garden was bathed in light.

And there stood Kitta, Professor Dement, Al and Tanglemoth. They waved up to her.

Felicity had never felt so happy, a stupid grin glued to her lips. Although the imp and the spindlysloth had taken a terrible risk coming to England, even at night. She hoped they would get back to Eternus okay and not be spotted. If they did, they'd probably be shipped off to a circus.

She wondered idly why Tantalus had not popped to see her too. Probably in his shop tallying up his gold and planning how to get even richer.

"So, we won?"

"We did," beamed the wizard. Then his eyes clouded over and the grin slipped off his lips. "But a lot of imps were injured..."

"But Al seems okay." She spotted he had on Wellington boots and a shockingly pink frilly dress. How stupid can stupid be?

"Yes, yes, he is, for him anyway. But the spindlysloths took a battering. Wizards too. I have bad news."

"Kitta's been horribly scared?" she asked hopefully.

"No. Sorry to say, Tantalus was murdered."

Felicity's lips formed an 'O'. She gulped. "But how?" she croaked.

"Remember Jumble Mud? Cheery chap, always helping blind kids, feeding stray kittens."

Felicity mustered a tiny grin. "Very funny." The dorfmoron was a terrifying monster, a killer and, on top of that, had terrible BO.

"Jumble Mud murdered him. He shoved a sword in his chest." Hickory looked at her and frowned. "I always thought you hated Tantalus."

"I did. He was always being nasty to me..." She stopped, remembering what Galibrath had told her. "But in the end he was okay. He was just a bit jumbled up."

The wizard rubbed his bristly chin. "Funny that."

"Funny ha-ha? Or just funny?"

Grinning, Hickory wheeled her back over to the bed. He swiped a HobNob and took a nibble. "I guess you grew on him."

"Like a fungus," mumbled Felicity, trying to sit up and scowling. Her left knee was throbbing and she felt her happy mood rapidly slipping away. "Anyway, why do you say that?"

Then, the wizard dropped his bombshell. "Because he left you The Wishing Shelf in his will."

I own The Wishing Shelf! Me! Felicity Brady! A BOSS!!! Al will be happy. Not! Tantalus left it to me but I wonder why. I thought he hated me. Must be my magical charm and sparkling eyes.

Poor old Tantalus. I feel bad. I told him to kill a troll to impress Kitta. No, not my fault. What if I had told him to jump off a cliff? Feel bad anyway. Maybe next time I visit Galibrath, I will see him too. I can say sorry and thank him for giving me the shop.

But do I want it? I need to go to school every day but I guess The Clock by the Door will help a bit. I can invite authors in to sign books, maybe even Professor E Gomorrha. I know! A coffee morning and a Top Ten list.

JUST HAD A FANTASTIC IDEA! Al can run a kids' club. He'll love that.

Wonderful to see Hickory. He kissed me on the cheek for two and a half seconds. I counted. He seems happy. Kitta's okay too, and Dement.

He returned my diary too. I thought I had lost it. Sort of wish I had. If Hickory looked in it he now knows I think Kitta is a nutter and that I want to marry him.

How embarrassing!

Chapter 3

Stop Scoffing All My HobNobs

Felicity's days were now filled with doctors telling her to 'Try harder', 'Swallow this', and to stop hiding her semolina pudding in her bedpan. Her legs were still hidden in the thick casts but they were now covered in autographs and silly drawings of sheep and furry monsters. (Lucy, a pal from school, had popped in. She had always been very good at art). Her mum had even had a go and drawn a bird's nest fern.

She loved potted plants.

Her legs did not kill her so much now but they did itch like crazy, so her dad had presented her with a knitting needle so she could scratch her ankle.

One Saturday morning, Felicity was sitting up in bed trying to stretch her legs, when she got the biggest shock of her life.

"A glass of warm milk, luvvy?" A nurse, wheeling a trolley, asked her.

She looked up and yelped. It was Bartholomew Banks, the goblin.

"Barf?!" she croaked, her thoughts swirling in her mind like socks in a tumble dryer.

"Banks," the goblin muttered sourly. "The name is Banks." He nabbed a HobNob off her table.

The last time she had seen the annoying goblin had been in Lupercus Castle. He had been bitten by a wolf and Felicity had thought he had been killed. He was a bit of a rascal and she did not trust him. The fact he looked so blooming ugly did not help. He had lots and lots of saggy chins, bushy 'caterpillar' eyebrows and the soft shiny skin of a python. Felicity had never seen a bigger hooter than the goblin's. In fact, if he entered it in a banana growing contest, he'd sweep to victory. However, he was the best dressed goblin she had ever met, and she had met a lot. But not today, for he had on a matron's uniform and from under his white hat sprang a mop of golden locks.

"I like the wig," she kidded him. "Must feel odd not being a baldy."

Banks pursed up his lips. "Thanks for that."

"Sorry. Anyway, I thought..."

"I had kicked the bucket? No way," the goblin boasted, giving her a hyena smirk. "No stinking wolf is gonna get rid of me. But I did see a long, black tunnel and my old granny. She looked to be knitting a green jumper." He rested his cheek on his shoulder. "Odd that. She hated green - and knitting."

Felicity rolled her eyes. The goblin did talk a lot of gibberish.

"But you had a big gash in your neck and you were bleeding really badly."

"Shift up a bit, fatty." To Felicity's horror, Banks squeezed up next to her and stretched out his legs. The man in the next bed was asleep but what if Doctor Besaggy walked by, or a nurse?

He snatched a second HobNob. Felicity gritted her teeth. Greedy goblin.

"Don't get crumbs in my bed," she warned him, buttoning up her top button. She wished she had hidden them under her pillow.

He ignored her. "So, there I was, lying on the floor, my new Yves Saint Laurent shirt drenched in blood. Very difficult to get out. Mind you, Daz is very good. 'Black blacker than black'. I did the doorstep challenge, you know. Anyway, lots of WANDD agents showed up, thought I had been killed too. They even wanted to stuff me and stick me in Twice Brewed Museum. But I snuck away, popped to hospital, a shot of dragon's milk and a bed bath off Matron Bendalot, Bob's y' uncle."

Felicity looked disgruntled. "Why was I not taken to the hospital in Eternus? A spot of magic, a bed bath off -," she frowned, eyeing him doubtfully, "- is that actually her name?"

Banks tittered. "Much better to be with your family, I think." His lips curled under. "I only wish my mum and dad had dropped in to see me."

"You had a mum and dad!? I thought you jumped out of a bubbling cauldron or the jaws of a dragon or a big green lizard."

The goblin punished her by grabbing a third HobNob. "Anyway, try a drop of this." He handed her a tiny green bottle, a cork jammed in the top. "Rub it on your bum and toes every night. I can help, if you like," he added with a leer.

Turning it over and over in her hand, Felicity looked at it doubtfully.

"Okay, okay, you got me. Only kidding. Just your bum. Fix you up in a jiffy."

He clambered to his feet, looking bored. She watched him wander over to the next bed. "Look at the size of his boobs," he observed. "You could twist 'em up and make a balloon poodle." He snatched up the chart from off the end of the fat man's bed, conjured up a feathery pen and began to scribble on it.

Felicity looked on, aghast. "Er, evil goblin, should you really be doing that?"

"Why not? This man needs help. Stupid doctors. Says here he needs twenty pills a day. Wrong! No trophy! No gold medal! What he

needs is," he wrote as he talked, "locking – in –
a – room – and – feeding – lettuce – for – two –
months. There we go!" He signed it, "Nurse
Banks," and hung it back on the hook.

"So, planning to pop to Eternus soon? The
landlady of the Ye Olde Banshee pub told me
that Tantalus left you The Wishing Shelf in
his will."

Felicity shrugged, looking glum.

"What's up with you?"

"Why were you talking about me to the
landlady of the pub?"

Banks crossed his eyes and smirked. "Did I
say we were talking?"

Felicity grunted and rubbed her tired eyes.
"Look, since I stumbled on The Wishing
Shelf, demons, dorfmorons and nasty wizards
have been trying to murder me. Now, my knee
is shattered, a disgusting monster's finger is
hanging off my big toe, every hour I need to
rub jelly on my bottom and, on top of that, I
met you."

"Bla, bla, bla. Stop being so crabby, Brady."
He scowled. "Why the monster's finger
anyway? Is it a shubablybub's?"

"Yes, it is." A smug look hung off her lips. "Hickory got it for me…"

Banks interrupted her by chanting, "Felicity and Hickory sitting in a tree, K – I – S – S – I – N – G."

"Stop it! Everybody is trying to sleep. Anyway, better to kiss a hot wizard than a goblin with twenty-seven chins," Felicity retorted.

Banks' lower lip trembled.

"Oh, did I upset you?" she added, grinning. Teasing the goblin was not just fun, it was a very important part of her life. "Anyway," she shrugged, "I just feel tired of - everything."

"Hey, Brady, life is messy, not just full of yo-yos, Twix bars and that silly girls sport, you know, with the net and the ball."

"Er, netball?"

"Yeah, that's it."

Twiddling her thumbs, Felicity looked lost in thought. "Did you bring me a Twix, then?"

Banks threw up his hands in disgust. "The Wishing Shelf is a wonderful shop, full of wonderful exciting books. Hedes Spine is just a joke now Tantalus is six feet under." He grinned at this and danced a bit of a jig. Felicity remembered how he had hated the wizard. "You now own the only bookshop in Twice Brewed."

As the goblin spoke, Felicity's eyes grew wider and wider. "Crikey Banks, did you just try and lift my spirits? You - being a nasty, evil, blood-thirsty goblin who kills tiny kittens and baby hamsters for a job?"

Banks' cheeks blossomed cherry-pink. "It's not a job, it's a hobby. And I enjoy jumping on frogs too. Such a wonderful popping sound." Looking nasty, he snatched up the chart off the end of her bed. "Multi-fracturing of the tibias," he read, "and crushed patella of the left leg." He grunted. "What is all that?"

"The big bone is broken here, here, here, here, here, here and here, and this kneecap," she prodded her left leg, "now looks a lot like scrambled eggs."

"Nasty!"

"It is. In fact, my doctor is planning to box my legs up and sell them as a jigsaw puzzle."

For a very, VERY short second, the goblin looked ALMOST sorry for her. Then he shrugged and felt for the pen. "Cut - off - all - her," he mumbled as he scribbled. He looked up. "Is there an 'e' in toes?"

"Barf, you nut bar!"

Chuckling wickedly, he hooked the chart back on the end of the bed. They glared at each other, then the goblin's eyes slowly shifted to the HobNobs.

"No!" Felicity bellowed, diving for the packet, but the goblin was just too quick for her. She watched in dismay as he snatched up her 'tiny bit of joy', snapped his fingers and vanished.

Over in the next bed, the obese man yelped like a scared puppy. "D-did that nurse just - y' know, in a ball of green smoke?"

Felicity nodded, showing him the palms of her hands. "Yep. She nicked my HobNobs."

The shaking man seemed to shrink in his pyjamas and ducked under the sheets.

"Doctor!" came a muffled cry, "I need a stronger sleeping pill."

Chapter 4

Baggy, Egg-Yolk Yellow Dinosaur Pyjamas

 "INCREDIBLE!"

"Amazing!"

"Holy cow!"

The three doctors, clustered around the end of her bed, were all gawping at her legs in wonder. Felicity's cheeks glowed London-bus red. She felt like she was in the circus. Soon, lots of kids holding sticks of candyfloss would run up and pay a pound to laugh at her.

Ironically, if a month or so ago a trio of men had eyed up her legs, she would have been doing cartwheels. But a month or so ago her legs were not a road map of horrid purple scars.

Ironically, her cartwheeling days were over too.

She watched as Doctor Besaggy prodded her left knee and scratched his head. She could just tell them. But she pictured Doctor Besaggy's face on being told, 'I hung a shubablybub finger on my big toe, oh, and every day I rub green jelly on my bottom.' Best to keep her trap shut or they would just stick her in the mental ward.

"I took all my pills," she piped up meekly, "and my dad brings me a bottle of milk every day. Helps the bone to mend," she added lamely, "so dad reckons."

Hidden under the sheets, Felicity wrung her hands as the doctors mulled over her chart. "A remarkable recovery," Doctor Besaggy announced at last, his bushy eyebrows climbing his head. They looked like caterpillars racing to get to the top.

Felicity shot up in bed. "Can I go home now!?" She was getting bored of sleeping all day, mushy peas and stodgy rice pudding.

Besaggy shrugged. "The X-rays show your legs and knee have mended - in only ten days." His eyes narrowed, his twitch working ten to the dozen, as if he suspected her of tampering with the charts clutched in his hands.

Felicity felt her face burn even redder, but she bit back the urge to develop her 'milk drinking' story.

She watched the doctors huddle up at the end of her bed like players in a really weedy rugby team. If only they would let her go home. She missed Sam and her room and her dad's bangers and mash.

"Okay, Felicity," the doctors' heads split apart, "get a good night sleep and you can go home tomorrow morning. But you must keep doing your therapy. Lots of walking and stretching. No lying in bed all day watching silly TV and playing Pac Man."

Wondering idly what Pac Man was, Felicity nodded ardently.

She watched them amble up the ward, still discussing the wonder of her legs. She grimaced. They did not look too wonderful to her. All jagged scars and blackened skin. She was destined to a life of jeans, long skirts and romantic lighting.

Whoopee!

"So how do you feel today, Mrs Bartok? Your head still throbbing?"

Besaggy's herd of sheep had stopped by the old lady in the far corner of the ward. She never talked, even to the doctors, and she always seemed to be crying. To Felicity, she looked drowned in her baggy, egg-yolk yellow dinosaur pyjamas and she had a greenish tint to her skin. She could tell by the look on Doctor Besaggy's face that she was very poorly.

When the doctors finally left the ward, Felicity, full of the joy of going home, made up her mind to go and visit the sad old lady. Maybe, she could cheer her up a bit, tell her a funny story. Yesterday, her dad had told her a super funny joke about a vicar, a cage of monkeys and a jar of Marmite.

Gingerly, she clambered off her bed, grabbed up a crutch and hobbled up the ward. Her knee still hurt a lot but not in a 'KILL ME! END MY MISERY!' sort of way. She got to the lady's bed and pulled up a chair. On it, there was a 'Hello' magazine, different to her mum's, the front cover telling the world why George Clooney was so hot, and how a pop star had overdosed on Botox.

She'd have to read that. Shifting the magazine to the floor, she gingerly sat down.

"Hello, I'm Felicity."

Slowly, the old wrinkly lady opened her eyes and looked at her. "Let me be, child." Her cheeks were wet. She had been crying.

"Oh, okay. I, er, just thought you might want to chat a bit. It can get a bit lonely in here."

"No." She shut her eyes, ending the debate.

Crikey! This was going well. "You know, we have identical pyjamas on."

The old lady frowned, then, begrudgingly, the corners of her mouth twitched up. "Yes, I guess we do. My name is Mrs Bartok." She waved a lazy hand at Felicity's legs. "How did you hurt them? Took a nasty tumble? Fell off your bike?"

Felicity looked at her and suddenly felt tired of telling untruths. "A bonkers wizard pushed a shelf of books on me," she announced matter-of-factly. "My legs got all crushed and broken."

"Not a very nice chap."

"He's dead."

"Did you kill him? Or did your dad? I spotted him yesterday in a uniform. Is he in the army?"

"Yes. And no, Bogsnark did. He's a gargoyle."

Mrs Bartok sat up gingerly in her bed and hooked her hands on her knees. "I do love a good story. Tell me everything."

So she did. She told her all about The Wishing Shelf, the talking books and the old wizard who had let her work there, about Articulus, the evil book that had been swiped first by a demon and then by the fiendish wizard, Incantus Gothmog. She told her about fighting on a rope bridge, her crush on Hickory Crowl, and being chased by night demons and dorfmorons. She even told her about Al, the imp, and the nasty teas he brewed. She felt so much better getting it all off her chest.

The old lady's eyes danced. "What a wonderful story, Felicity. Magic is so exciting. And you got to see this old wizard in a room in the clouds, you say? You actually chatted to him?"

"Yes, I did."

A tear trickled down her cheek. "Maybe, when I pop off, I will get to see my old Henry." She sighed. "He was such a trooper. Always making things in his shed or up on the roof fixing the chimney pot."

Feeling embarrassed, Felicity suddenly found her pink slippers to be absolutely fascinating. "I hope so too," she mumbled.

Rallying a smile, Mrs Bartok rested her grey curls back on the hill of pillows. "Years ago, when I was fourteen, just a spotty teenager really..." She glanced at Felicity. "No offense."

Felicity smiled ruefully, shaking her head.

"Anyway, my dad took me to a magic show at the Royal. So posh, all gilt and velvet. We went in his Ford Cortina. Amazing, it was." She chuckled. "The magic show, not the Cortina. Fantasio the Great! He sawed his wife in half. I read in the paper they got divorced soon after. I clapped till my hands were raw..."

Stuffing her chilly fingers in her armpits, Felicity stretched out her poorly legs and settled back to listen.

Mrs Bartok did not wake up this morning. They covered her over. Her son popped in but he only stayed ten seconds to collect her stuff.

Poor lady. But I think she enjoyed my story. I do hope she finds her Henry.

Banks visited me yesterday. Charming as ever! He had on a long golden wig. Wish I had my camera. He nabbed all my HobNobs too. What a fatty.

Tired of rubbing green jelly on my bottom. Maybe it is just jelly and Banks is laughing at me, but too scared to stop doing it now. Anyway, the shubablybub finger seems to be doing the trick.

Keep seeing monsters in my sleep. All torn flesh and burnt skin. Oh, and hoofs for feet. Disgusting things.

WONDERFUL, WONDERFUL NEWS!!! Teddy popped in to see me and he asked me to go to the cinema with him. A DATE! AT LAST! And I got a box of mint twiggler-thingys off him too. He is sooooo sweet!

Chapter 5

A Torrent of Poo Adjectives

Felicity stood for a moment by the door to The Wishing Shelf, remembering how she had first stumbled upon the bookshop. She had been chased by a gang of hooligans from her school. She had hidden by the bridge but when the boys had spotted her, the kind old shop had offered her sanctuary.

She had no clue what the Secret Saying of the Day was, so she'd have to knock. Balancing on a crutch, she rapped sharply on the wooden door. It was only ten in the morning, so Al, the imp, was probably still tucked up in his cot; that or brewing a cuppa.

"Open up," she called.

Maybe Hickory and Kitta were in the bookshop by now. Better yet, maybe only Hickory.

Balancing dangerously on the crutch, Felicity rubbed her mittened hands and stuffed them in her pockets. Blooming freezing! Then the door cracked open and a mop of crazy curls popped out.

The imp!

Only three feet tall, he had twigs for legs and dustbin lids for feet. His podgy cheeks hid under a nest of freckles and his ears stuck up like Spock's on Star Trek. Felicity spotted he had on Kitta's slippers and a long yellow gown covered in penguins. They looked to be sitting on the tops of icebergs, chomping fish.

He rubbed his eyes sleepily, then plonked on a bobbly pink hat, hiding his ears. "We don't open till twelve...ish," he grumbled to her left knee.

Felicity's eyes grew wide. "Twelve!?" she echoed.

"Yep." He yawned and scratched his bottom. "Now I'm the big boss I need my shut eye."

"But…"

The imp shook a gangly finger at her. "Talk to the hand, baby doll." He began to shut the door but Felicity slipped the end of her crutch in the gap.

"Oy! Look up. Remember me? Felicity?"

The imp's jaw dropped to his chest. "FELICITY!" Skipping out of the shop, he hugged her legs.

Felicity grinned and patted his bobbly hat warmly, trying to ignore the throbbing in her poor knee.

"So, now we open at twelve?" she quizzed him, rapping her knuckle on his head.

Pulling away, the imp had the decency to look to his big feet. "So I get a chance to do all the dusting," he managed lamely.

Felicity rolled her eyes. "Good idea," she teased him. "Every year or so to keep your hand in." She pushed at the door but it had already shut. "Al, what's the Secret Saying of the Day?"

Frowning, the imp scratched his hat. "Hmm, tricky that," he mumbled.

"Al!"

"Okay! Okay! Keep y' teeth in. I remember I was sitting on the loo when I thought of it. He leant on the door. "Smelly poo! No. Stinky poo! No..."

Felicity looked up at the sky. So much for being the proud owner of The Wishing Shelf. She could not even open the front door.

"To call you stupid," she mumbled, "would be an insult to stupid people."

The imp ignored her. "Pongy poo! No. Putrid poo! No. Can I cut a small flap in the door?"

Felicity shook her head firmly.

So, like lemons, they stood there, the imp reciting a torrent of poo adjectives at the stubborn door. Sadly, but for the imp, the shop had been empty. It seemed that Kitta and Hickory had popped back to Kitta's cottage up in the hills by Cauldron City.

Felicity's feet and fingers were bitterly cold and having to hand over her socks and mittens to the imp had not helped matters. Why did he have to be such a baby? Resting her shoulder on the grimy window, she watched him in annoyance. She guessed there was no real hurry. Easter holidays had just begun so no school for two weeks, but she did have a lot of studying to do, to catch up. Her maths teacher, Miss Stern, had popped into the hospital and had presented her with a fat book of sums. She needed to go back to school just for a holiday.

Suddenly, a portly man bumbled down the steps and stopped in front of her. He pulled off his bowler hat and bowed. "Mayor Glumweedy of Twice Brewed," he introduced himself, "I got 27,522 votes. Bethany Butterlygum got 252. Kicked her butt. And you must be Felicity Brady. How do you do?"

She nodded dumbly and shook his squidgy hand. She took him to be a wizard – always tell by the eyes - but if so, what was he doing in England?

"Not going in?" he inquired, looking over at the door. "Well, it is a very sunny day."

Scowling, Felicity glanced up at the cloudy sky. It had begun to drizzle and she felt colder than a naked Eskimo sunbathing in Alaska in March.

Pretending to be Tarzan, the wizard slapped his fists on his chest. "Fill up the lungs, hey? Keep away that nasty Sleepy Eyelid Bug." Suddenly, he stopped slapping and whispered, "I was hoping to have a quick chat."

Felicity glared over at the imp who was thumping wildly on the door and bellowing, "STEAK AND KIDNEY! PORK! APPLE WITH A FLAKY CRUST!"

"So, it's a pie?"

But the imp just shrugged and started listing different sorts of puddings.

"Sorry about this," Felicity apologised to Glumweedy. "My imp is not too smart."

Glumweedy tittered. "Indeed, indeed. I can stuff him for you, if you want?"

"Er," Felicity wrinkled up her nose, "maybe later." Not knowing why, she felt annoyed that this wizard so willingly agreed with her. It was okay for *her* to insult Al, but not a stranger who kept grinding his teeth and smelt a tiny bit of a bacon and egg fry up.

He curled a chubby finger and beckoned her over to the fence by the river. Reluctantly, she followed him on her crutch.

"What happened to your legs?" he interrogated her, glaring at her knees.

"I, er…"

"I was told by a hag in Ye Olde Banshee pub that you now own The Wishing Shelf."

Felicity nodded curtly. What a rude man. But there was no way of escaping him. Not on a crutch and Al being such a blithering idiot. She glanced over at the imp in exasperation.

"I have a very important offer for you." Felicity chewed on her bottom lip so he soldiered on. "I want to buy The Wishing Shelf. A young, may I say, pretty girl like you should not be hiding away in a smelly bookshop. You should be out with your pals…"

"The Wishing Shelf is not for sale." She attempted to sound convincing but she could not help but wonder how much better her life would be if she got away from the bookshop. There was so much responsibility, so much to do and what had it ever given her? A headache, a sloppy goblin kiss, two broken legs and a crushed knee.

The chubby wizard smirked, detecting her sudden lack of gusto. "Go on a safari, get a bit of sun," he persisted. He plonked a sack by her feet. It clinked invitingly. Felicity scratched her chin, wondering where he had hidden it. "127 diamonds, 62 emeralds and a ruby the size of Jupiter's moons. Surprise your dad, buy him a Rolls Royce. Eat caviar." His cheeks burned red. "GET A LIFE!"

"Bangers and mash," bellowed Al, shouldering open the stubborn door. "I remember now, sitting on the loo, thinking of food..."

Felicity nodded to the wizard. "Thanks, but no thanks." She hobbled after the imp, but Glumweedy had not given up and followed her.

Once in the shop, the wizard shrugged and handed her a scroll. It was dripping wet. "You had better have a butchers at this, then."

Gently, not wanting to rip it, Felicity unrolled the soggy parchment.

"If, by the end of next week, I can get more wizards and hags to sign my scroll than you can, I get the shop anyway." He nudged her sharply in the ribs. "And I have over a hundred and ten already. Now, let me see, can

I squeeze a cupboard in by the door over there?" A ruler jumped out of his pocket. "Ooh, what a horrid looking sofa. That will need to go." He wandered off through the shop.

Felicity plonked her bottom on the sofa next to the toy rabbit Tantalus had left there the day he had been killed. She felt as if the sun had packed its bags and left for a long holiday to Manchester.

Reluctantly, she looked over to the imp. She was probably going to regret this. She shrugged. "So champ, what we going to do now?"

For a split second, she thought she spotted tiny teapots dancing in his eyeballs. "A cuppa is excellent for the noggin," he told her. He snapped his fingers and vanished in a puff of pinkish mist. Felicity rubbed her eyes. The imp could always be counted on in a crisis; counted on to go and pop the kettle on.

Wishing he had bribed Ratchet to do this crazy stunt, Glumweedy crept through the bookshop. "ANYBODY THERE?!" he called. "I GOT A TASTY SNACK HERE!" He had a porkchop crushed in his fist, blood dripping onto his cufflink.

Maybe the monster did not exist. Maybe the old hag in the pub who had told him had just been trying to scam him.

A myth, perhaps.

A legend.

Smirking in the gloom, he remembered how he had pretended to go to the loo in the pub and then slipped away. He had not even had to cough up for the hag's drink.

Glumweedy yelped. In front of him, a small monster had just jumped off a shelf. Brandishing the porkchop like a crucifix, the wizard tossed it to him.

So, there *is* still a woolly glumsnapper in The Wishing Shelf, thought Glumweedy in delight. He's not just a myth after all.

Scared of alarming him, the wizard kept very still. Slowly, the elaborate untruths he had planned to say formed on his lips. "Must be, er, awfully lonely in here." On his knees, the monster ignored him, chomping on the slab of pork. "Odd though, there being so many glumsnappers left in Twice Brewed."

Coughing up the chop and splattering a book, the monster growled and jumped to his chicken-like feet.

Hastily, Glumweedy backpedaled, but all too soon his bottom smacked the shop wall. The tiny monster darted up to him, his googly eyes level with the wizard's belly button. "Yep, er, lots and lots of woolly glumsnappers," Glumweedy gasped, trying to recover, "but sadly, that Brady-girl, who owns the shop; she will not let them in. Selfish, I call it."

Snarling, the monster wiped a splatter of blood off his chin with his foot.

"Sh-sh-shocking, hey?" the wizard stumbled. "But if, say, the shop had nobody in it buying books, she'd be forced to sell it - to me."

The monster stepped away, looking puzzled.

Slowly, Glumweedy felt his greed overcoming his fear. "Oh, did I tell you, I love woolly glumsnappers."

Two hours later, Felicity was slumped on the sofa listening in horror to Al's tale of life in The Wishing Shelf on his own.

"Wonderful!" bawled the imp, jumping up on her lap. "Just wonderful! I had been trying to sleep in till 10 o'clock but customers kept knocking on the door, disturbing me. Very annoying. So I plugged my ears with candle wax and 'Bob's y' uncle!' now a fog horn can't wake me. Tomorrow, I was planning not to get up at all."

"Al, you turnip!" Felicity fumed, shoving the imp off her knees, but Al was saved from a proper good telling-off by the door to the shop bursting open and a uniformed gnome marching in. He had on a cap, a long baton clutched in his hand.

Fidget Moth!

The last time Felicity had seen the feisty little fellow, he had been on his way to fight in the battle for Lupercus Castle.

"Wotcha," uttered Felicity. Al had put her in a bad mood and the gnome looked way too cheerful. "You survived the battle, then."

Fidget Moth saluted her smartly, whipped off his cap and slipped it in his armpit. "Slayed a nasty troll and a dragon too. AND I got a shiny medal." He lifted up the lapel of his jacket and showed it to her.

Felicity nodded. "Good work."

"Order of the Yellow Unicorn. My mum, bless her, bawled all the way through the ceremony."

Humming a ditty and looking annoyingly smug, Glumweedy strutted by them. He reminded Felicity of a dog who had just dug up a juicy bone. "Got everything I needed," he called smugly over his shoulder. "Now, I can pop and get carpets and a rug for the loo. "Oooh," he snapped his fingers, "and I must hire a skip to lob all the old books in."

The shop full of books gasped in horror.

Glaring after his wobbly buttocks, Felicity jumped to her feet. "You cheeky lump of lardy..." but sadly, her string of highly original insults was interrupted by a blood-curdling growl.

The room shuddered, the window cracking, scoring a lightning bolt in the glass. Yelping, the 'Witch Spotter's' book tumbled off her shelf to the floor.

Sitting up, she rubbed her spine. "I just had a ghastly nightmare," she grumbled. "A frog-eyed monster in a pink apron with ducks on it kept munching on my turnip. But I kept telling him, 'It's not ripe yet'." She shrugged. "Very odd. Very, very odd indeed."

Chapter 6

Lumps of Square Coal and the Sleepy Eyelid Bug

Watching a goldfish lazily circling a tank, Felicity decided even in Eternus waiting rooms were boring. She hunched up her shoulders to try and stay warm. There was not even a poster on the wall of a girl in a skimpy bikini selling fake tan, or even a 'Smoking Kills' sign. Felicity was perched on a cold bench and Al was sitting next to her. He was cold too. She could hear his teeth chattering. Over in a corner, a wizard in a kilt and really long socks was browsing through a crumpled copy of 'Wizards Weekly'. He was chuckling. Maybe, she mused, he was reading the problem page. A shaggy dog was curled up by his feet. He kept yapping and pedalling his paws; probably dreaming of rabbits.

She glanced up. Circling her head was the number 27. Round and around it skidded, sending up misty wisps, like socks left on a rock to dry. A yellow parrot with red feet and a shocking green mohican lolled on a beam in the roof. It had just screeched '26'.

Her turn next.

Feeling bored and not wanting to read, 'Classic Carpets Monthly', she nudged the imp. "Flippin' freezing in here," she grumbled, blowing in her hands. "Do wizards even know what a radiator is?"

The imp waved a reprimanding finger in her face and snootily told her to, "Shush!" and "Show a bit of respect." He passed her a card a witch had handed to him on the way in. Felicity read it:

DO NOT

1. Chatter, sneeze, cough, snore, belch or hiccup.

2. Smell of liquorice, corned beef or dragon dung.

3. Teach the parrot vulgar limericks (she knows most of them anyway).

4. Try to bribe the parrot with hazelnuts to get to the front of the queue.

5. We could not think of a number 5 but you must not, under any circumstances, invent your own.

The wizard in the corner lit up a pipe and Felicity wondered idly why sneezing was banned but it was okay to smoke.

"27," squawked the bird.

Still circling her, the number 27 shot off, slowly shrivelling up like a 'let off' balloon. It hit a cactus in the window and popped.

Quickly, she stood up and smoothed down her brown skirt. She had on a floppy jumper she had borrowed from her mum and she had polished her school boots. She hoped she looked okay. She even had on eyeliner and a rustic-looking braclet. She thought, being the owner of a magical bookshop, she'd try and look a little older. And wiser!

She padded over to a hatch whilst the parrot amused the room with a performance of 'There was a young impster from Peru, who escaped a high security zoo'. There, she was directed down a plush corridor to a door fit for a giant. On it, in bold glossy letters, was a sign.

THE PLANNING OFFICE
'We plan, so you can'

"Shall I knock?" she quizzed Al who had followed her. He was busy licking his palms and trying to flatten down the unruly curls on his head and toes. He had put on his best linen shorts and on his t-shirt he had scribbled,

MR RATCHET FOR KING

Felicity had no clue who Mr Ratchet was.

The imp had led her to the Planning Office but only after she had bribed him with three mugs of fudge and fig tea, a jam doughnut and a packet of Cheesy Wotsits. He still had a blob of jam on his chin but she decided not to tell him.

Al nodded. "This is the Planning Office," he admonished her in a very lordly way, puffing out his weedy chest. "You knock, bow, curtsey, flip a cartwheel and hoola if they ask you to."

Felicity did not have a hoop on her and her legs hurt too much to flip a cartwheel. She decided just to knock. Maybe she would curtsey later.

"ENTER!" The shout shook the door in its frame.

Felicity slowly twisted the bronze handle and shouldered open the door. She stepped in, the imp crowding her heels. The planning office was very big and very, very tidy. VERY, VERY TIDY! Old books lined the walls and a coal fire helped by a window lit the room. Felicity gawped at the fire and blinked. The lumps of coal were cube-shaped and the flames were perfect pyramids. In the very middle of the room there was a mahogany desk and sitting at it was a wizard. A skinny stick of a man, he had trophy-sized lugs, and was so ugly she'd prefer to go on a date with Banks. He was scribbling in a ledger but looked up irritably as she gently shut the door.

"Do you have a slot, miss?" he demanded.

A plump book, balanced on a filing cabinet behind his left shoulder, flipped open. Calmly, it informed the office, "Grand Duke Franz Figglewick is expected at 10 o'clock."

The wizard looked Felicity up and down. "There's no way you are the Grand Duke. He's over three hundred years old, he drinks blood, he has a pet poodle called Flea and he has fangs the size of bananas." He glanced down at the ledger he'd been writing in. "I see here he wants to extend his cemetery and build three new crypts. We shall see if he has deep pockets..."

"Nope," piped up Felicity. She had to stop him or risk yawning. Annoyingly, the wizard kept shutting his eyes when he talked and when he did open them he seemed to be looking over her head.

The wizard scowled and placed his pencil on the desk next to a feathery quill and a wooden ruler. They were so neatly lined up they looked like cutlery in a posh restaurant. "No, no slot or no to being the Grand Duke?"

"Both. Sir," she added to be polite.

"Hmm." Scratching his ear, he pulled open a drawer in his desk. "Fill this in," he instructed her, waving a sheet of paper at her. "Black ink, capitals, no smudges, no scribbles, no doodles. I will try and see you in the next three months and," he consulted a calendar on his desk, "seven days."

Felicity's chin hit her chest. "But in three months and seven days it will be too late," she protested.

"Why? Are you dying? There's a lot of that going around." All of a sudden, he pulled back, his hand over his face. "Have you got the Sleepy Eyelid Bug?"

"I don't think so."

"Check your tongue, do you have spots on it? Have you any warts on your big toe?"

Oddly, she did have a verruca.

"I had the Sleepy Eyelid Bug," murmured Al, tugging at the hem of her mum's jumper. He had a dreamy look on his face. "Best bug ever, slept for a week."

Felicity ignored him. "I do not have the Sleepy Eyelid Bug," she insisted, "but I do own The Wishing Shelf. I got this letter..."

"You must be Felicity Brady," the wizard suddenly gushed. He jumped up, ushering her over to his desk. A stool dashed over and nudged the back of her legs. She collapsed onto it. The man tutted and yanked the stool to the left so that it was central to the desk.

The imp stood meekly next to her. Felicity wondered why he did not get a stool too.

Sitting back down, he leant on his desk, slipping his balled-up fists under his chin. "So, Miss Brady, my name is Mr Ratchet. How can I be of help to you? Remember, I plan, so you can."

Felicity glanced at Al's t-shirt. So, this was Mr Ratchet; and the poor imp still had to stand up!

She decided to jump in at the deep end. "Tantalus Falafel left me The Wishing Shelf in his will but now a fat geezer called Fester Glumweedy is trying to get his podgy hands on it. Can he do that?"

"No, no, no." Ratchet chuckled in an annoying way. But then the grin froze on his face and he shrugged. "Yes, he can. The problem is, Felicity, can I call you Felicity? Good. I had a cat called Felicity," it suddenly dawned on him, "always piddling on the sofa." He frowned at her as if concerned she might have a similar problem and pee on the stool. "Anyway, there's a law, a new law, in fact our mayor, Fester Glumweedy, introduced it only a few weeks ago..."

"Now there's a surprise," muttered Felicity, rolling her eyes.

Ratchet ignored her. "The law tells us, if a wizard pops off and has no kids and hands his property to a third party, then a different wizard, or witch, may fight them for it."

Felicity pulled a face. "Terrific," she sighed.

"Yes! Yes, it is." Buggingly, he was still shutting his eyes. "Which ever party gets the most wizards or hags to sign his or her scroll wins."

"So, if I get the most...?"

"You get to keep The Wishing Shelf." He cocked his thumb and shot her with his index finger. "Exactly."

He was so condescending, Felicity wanted to slowly murder him.

She shook her head in exasperation. "But, I got this silly letter." She unrolled it and waved it in the wizard's face. She no longer felt the need to be polite. "It says here in black ink, capitals, no smudges, no scribbles, no doodles," she added, sourly. "It says I only have two weeks. Can this be correct?"

"Only two weeks?" Ratchet echoed her. "I wonder why you did not get it sooner. I sent it by Imp Post. I remember slapping a stamp on his left buttock." Ratchet was not a very good liar. He slipped a finger in his collar and pulled it loose. "Is it hot in here, or is it just me?"

"I did not get it sooner," bristled Felicity, "because Fester Glumweedy had it. In fact, I think he had a bath with it. It was soaking wet.

"Did he now, the sly beggar. How odd." The wizard banged his fist feebly on the top of the desk. The pencil jumped and rolled away.

He snapped it up and popped it in his pocket. There were now two in there and Felicity wondered if it was a 'naughty pocket' where escapee pencils went. "Did you want to file a protest?" He snapped his fingers and the bottom drawer of the filing cabinet sprung open. "You'll need to fill in a lot of forms in black ink, capitals..."

Felicity jumped to her feet and rested her fists on the top of his desk. "How can I get lots of wizards and hags to sign my scroll, if I spend all week doing that?" she demanded angrily.

"Smart lass." Smirking, Ratchet nodded shrewdly. "Tell me," he suddenly whispered as if sharing the secret of Aladdin's cave with her, "do you happen to have a ton or two of gold in the bank?"

Looking confused, Felicity shook her head and flopped back onto the stool.

"A chest of emeralds then, or diamonds perhaps? Any will do."

"No."

"Silver spoons?"

"No."

"Silver forks?"

"No."

"Pity."

It was at this moment that Felicity decided that Mr Ratchet of the Planning Office was a wicked, greedy, sly baboon.

Accidently nudging the imp in the eye, she got up to go. But then a thought struck her. "Can only wizards and hags sign it?"

The wizard shot her a peculiar look. "Oh no, anybody can, but they will need the teeth for it," he chuckled, "or how can they?"

Felicity scowled, feeling annoyed. Teeth? Why teeth? How difficult is it to work a ruddy pen? But she did not get the opportunity to discuss it, for there was a terrific banging on the door.

Flapping wildly, the book on the filing cabinet bellowed, "ENTER!"

A very old man burst in. He had on a black bowler hat and a riding crop clutched in his hand. A tiny prancing poodle yapped by his feet.

"Duke," yelped Ratchet. "How wonderful to see you, old chap."

Trying to ignore his fangs and the feeling he saw her not so much as a young girl, but as a tasty pepperoni pizza, Felicity tiptoed over to him. "What a sweet dog." She patted his poodle. "By the way, I own The Wishing Shelf. I wonder, will you sign my scroll?"

Walked in The Wishing Shelf. Two seconds later, a fat geezer called Fester Glumweedy told me he's taking the shop off me.

Must be a record!

Seems I need to get lots and lots and LOTS of wizards to sign a scroll to say The Wishing Shelf stays The Wishing Shelf.

Al took me to the Planning Office in Eternus. Met a Mr Ratchet. What a plonker! Super plonker! But Duke Franz Figglewick signed my scroll. Well, he bit it anyway. Hey, if it works it works.

I think we may have a visitor in the shop. Not seen anything but whatever it is, it enjoys growling. That bonkers witch popped in, Matilda I think, to buy a book on poppodils. Odd thing is, I did not see her go.

Six days till date with Teddy. Need to buy a dress. Shall I go for the 'classy' look or the 'kiss me and let's swap chewing gum' look?

Called Lucy and Matilda yesterday to tell them. Lucy thinks the best way to get a kiss is to just kiss him.

BUT WHAT IF I MISS!?

Slept badly all week. Flesh-dripping monsters keep lurking in my mind, waking me up.

They frighten me.

Chapter 7

Wiring a Plug and a Chewed Biro

The first week in The Wishing Shelf passed by in a flash. Felicity, keen to show the doubting wizards of Twice Brewed her skills, spent almost every hour of every day in the shop, trying to put the books in order (annoyingly, they kept running away), writing letters to Professor E Gomorrha begging him to do a book signing (Imp Post, first class, stamp slapped on the buttock) and even erecting a pyramid of 'Ghouls, Not Just For Christmas' in the window. Even Al helped a tiny bit. Though, he did stop every hour, on the dot, to 'pop the kettle on' and to iron a few dozen t-shirts.

"Catch!" The imp tossed her a bunch of keys.

Felicity fingered them, frowning. "Why do I need keys? The door to the shop opens with the Secret Saying."

Today's was 'Jelly Baby and Honeycomb Swirls'. In memory of Galibrath, they always picked sweets.

"The owner of The Wishing Shelf always keeps the key ring," Al lectured her. "Every key is swim-ball-kick." Felicity suppressed a smile. She had a feeling he meant symbolic. "The bookshop has had twenty-seven owners, so the ring holds twenty-seven keys."

Most of the keys were crooked and a little rusty, but the biggest two looked all shiny and new.

She held one of them up. "Is this for me?"

"No, that was for Tantalus."

"Oh." Well, he had owned the bookshop, if only for a few weeks.

"The other is yours."

Perched on the desk, swinging her legs, Felicity looked shyly to the imp. "You cut this, just for me?"

"No, the handyman did it." The imp's chest swelled up. "But I told him to."

"Thanks." Then, flabbergasted, "We have a handyman!?"

"You bet, baby doll, but he's not very handy." The imp padded up to her and clicked his fingers. A mustard-yellow scroll jumped out of his shorts' pocket and unrolled. "By the way, I chatted to my lawyer..."

"A lawyer!?" mustered a gobsmacked Felicity, dropping the bunch of keys on the desk. "When did you get a lawyer?"

"Yesterday. I told him I had a different boss, a girl no less, and he sent me this list of demands. First, a turbo-charged teapot for the kitchen, my old teapot's missing; second, a two-way imp flap in the front door; third, a new cot; fourth, a fluffy blanket for Pyjamas, my cat; fifth..."

"How many demands do you have?" Felicity interrupted him, rubbing her brow and trying to ignore his exceedingly apt t-shirt,

I PUT THE ZZZZZZ IN LAZZZZZY

She had a headache coming on just over her left eye.

Squinting at the scroll, the imp announced grandly, "124. Fifth..."

"Hold on, Buster. "You need to help me sort Fester Glumweedy first or there may not be a Wishing Shelf to work in."

Reluctantly, the imp nodded, the scroll rolling up and diving up his sleeve. "Okay, but first you have to chat to the handyman."

"I do?"

"Yes," Al wrung his hands, "or how will he know who the boss is?"

Forgetting her poorly legs, Felicity jumped off the desk. "Okay," she winced, her bottom lip clamped in her teeth, "but how do I find him?"

The imp scampered over to the desk, took hold of a troll-shaped handle and pulled open the bottom drawer. Peering in warily, Felicity spotted a black lever and next to it, a list.

HAMMER (Only on Mondays after 11)
SCREW (Screws)
CUT (Only wood, no fleshy stuff)

SPRAY (No further than a foot)
CUPPA & A LONG NAP (Slurp & zzzz's)
MEET ME

"Simply drag the lever next to what you want him to do." Flexing his biceps, the imp yanked it next to the words, 'MEET ME'.

Instantly, The Wishing Shelf was filled with blasting sirens. In the roof, tiny red bulbs flashed on and off, and bats flew off the rafters in panic.

"What the heck...!?" shouted Felicity, ducking and covering her ears.

"He sleeps a lot," explained Al, "and very deeply too. Loggishly, in fact."

"So the handyman is as lazy as you?"

The imp blew a raspberry at her and slammed the drawer shut. The sirens stopped, the bulbs blinked off and the bats went back to sleep.

Twiddling her thumbs, Felicity lay sprawled on the sofa. She enjoyed being back in The Wishing Shelf, seeing all the old books and catching up on the gossip. The 'Witch Spotter's' book waddled over and told her that 'A History of Goblin Snot' had had a bit of hanky panky with 'Skin, Chop, Fry, How to Cook Dorfmoron Stew'.

"Interesting kids, I bet," the book chuckled, her cover flapping up and down.

BOOKS CAN HAVE KIDS!

Oooh! Not going there.

She lay there for two hours until, finally, the handyman showed up.

A SPINDLYSLOTH! Felicity rolled her eyes. They were sooooo slow.

Tall and wispy-looking, he had the soft eyes of a barn owl, all big and wary, and ruddy blotchy cheeks. Steel-capped hiking boots hid his ping-pong-bat sized feet and his fingers were long and bendy. He had on worn overalls and a tool belt hung off his hip like a cowboy's holster. Felicity stared at his frizzy locks in astonishment and wondered idly if he had just been wiring a plug.

"Just been wiring a plug," the handyman drawled.

"Wow!" Al smirked. "I bet that took…"

"Just over three days."

"A record for you."

Swelling up with pride, the spindlysloth nodded. "My fastest ever."

"A plug!?" Felicity scratched her chin. "But there's no electricity in The Wishing Shelf."

"No," agreed the handyman.

"No," agreed the imp.

"A bath plug," the handyman enlightened her.

"But how do you wire a bath plug?"

"Carefully," said the handyman.

"Carefully," said the imp.

Felicity scowled, her eyebrows knitting together. "So, hello." She shook his hand. "Felicity Brady, I'm the boss…"

"Where's old Douglas Falafel?" he interrupted her. Rather rudely, she thought.

The imp giggled. "He kicked the bucket a hundred and twelve years ago."

"Huh." The handyman stuffed his hands grumpily in his pockets. "Nobody told me."

"Anyway," persevered Felicity, "if you need anything, say a hammer, a screwdriver..." the handyman looked bored, "...or a er, drill," she faltered, remembering there was no electricity, "pop and see me."

He sniffed. "Will do."

"And the stools need fixing."

"Why?"

"Wobbly legs."

"Yes, and...?"

"And..." Vexed, she looked to Al.

"Every stool in The Wishing Shelf is wobbly," the imp told her. "That's the way it is."

"Why?"

He grinned moronically. "Sort of fun, in it? To wobble on them."

The handyman nodded slowly in agreement.

Rubbing her brow, Felicity watched the spindlysloth turn to go. Then she snapped her fingers. "I almost forgot. There may be a witch lost in the bookshop. If you spot her, help her to find the door."

The handyman reluctantly nodded. "Is that it, Boss?"

She looked over to the imp who showed her his palms and nodded. "Yep, I think so. Wonderful to meet you and er, thanks for popping by so er, promptly." Then, trying to be upbeat. "Keep wiring them plugs!"

Mumbling softly, he slouched off.

Felicity scowled. Did he just say, 'Bossy Boots'?

"By the way, Mr Handyman," she called after him, "can you fix the window?"

"So, that's not it," he grumbled, glancing over at the crack in the glass. "How did that happen?"

A blood-curdling cry echoed through The Wishing Shelf. A second lightning bolt scored the glass, answering the spindlysloth.

The spindlysloth frowned. "What's he doing up?"

"Who!?" Felicity dashed over to him. "Who's up?"

The handyman eyed her, looking puzzled. "I only see him in shadows and murky corners," he murmured darkly, and so slowly

Felicity wished she had a key to wind him up. "He's been here for well over a hundred years, I think. There were a lot of them back then but the first Incantus Gothmog got them all killed fighting for him. Every morning, I toss a chunk of liver and a carton of milk in the cellar. Keeps him fed, hey. He's not a bad sort."

Felicity looked on, gobsmacked. There really was a monster in her bookshop!

He bent over to study the crack in the glass, a Biro in the top pocket of his overalls falling to the floor. "Fix this up in a jiffy," he remarked.

"A jiffy being twelve months," joked the imp.

The handyman tittered and slumped over to the sofa. "How's this old thing doing? Still refusing to fly, hey? Gotta sort it."

Felicity's chin dropped to her chest. The sofa could fly!? Nobody told her anything.

"Sofa, up, up, up," he shouted, thumping it and giving it a good welly.

Slowly, the old sofa lifted up. A spring twanged and it tipped over, spilling books, a blanket and Pyjamas the cat onto the floor.

Pyjamas hissed and stalked off.

The handyman tutted. "Must fix that."

"Can you possibly stop feeding the monster," suggested Felicity awkwardly. She picked up the chewed pen. She hated giving orders.

The handyman shrugged and scratched his whiskery chin. "Okay, boss, but if I stop giving him food, what's he gonna eat?"

Felicity nodded enthusiastically. "Exactly. Then he may go away. Oh, and here's the Biro you dropped." She tossed it over to him.

Catching it niftily, he tossed it back to her. "Better keep it, hey lass." Then he turned to go, calling over his shoulder, "You will probably be needing it and I be thinking very, very soon."

A door in the far corner of the shop slammed shut.

Felicity turned to the imp and shot him a long, puzzled look. "Tell me, why do spindlysloths always talk utter rubbish?"

So, I went to see a film with Teddy. We got there a bit late so we had to watch 'Bloodthirsty Killer Spiders Attack Liverpool 2'. Not a classic film. The spiders acted the best. No Oscars there.

Annoyingly, Lucy and Matilda showed up. Wish I had never told them. They kept lobbing popcorn at us. So we got in a popcorn fight. I spilt 7up all over my dress and we got escorted from the cinema by security.

Now, the bad bit!

Teddy walks me to the front door. Good!

He held my hand. Good!

Then, HE KISSED ME! VERY, VERY, VERY GOOD!

Kiss was going very well.

Eyes shut.

Lips doing the 'goldfish' thing. He tasted a little of salty popcorn.

Out of nowhere, my dad walks up the path and shouts, "What's going on here?" Not so good!

I pulled away so quickly I cut my top lip on Teddy's teeth wire.

Long story short, dad sees blood and thinks Teddy hit me. Then he spots how wet my dress is. Suspects we went skinny-dipping.

I tell him, 'In March!? R u crazy!?'

Dad has a bit of a fit. Teddy scarpers, trips over dad's wheelbarrow, lands on his TEETH! And mum calls the ambulance. Classic!

Chapter 8

A Stampede of Hippos

Scowling, Ratchet wriggled a finger in his left ear. "Sorry, did you just say *you* handed the letter to the Brady-girl?"

Chomping on a bongeroo worm kebab, Glumweedy nodded, absentmindedly. "Just for a bit of sport, hey? Make it a challenge." A dollop of ketchup splattered on his lap. He wiped it up on the tip of his thumb and licked it off. "Anyway, there's not a drop of magic in her; she's just a silly little girl, and don't forget, I'm the most popular mayor in the history of Twice Brewed: 27,522 wizards and hags voted for me."

They were sitting on stools in the Droopy Wand Café discussing Glumweedy's plans for The Wishing Shelf. Well, most of them; not the secret stuff. The podgy wizard loved the café. They did the best fry up in Twice Brewed; dragon's egg, scrambled, baby stinky mushrooms and a tomato the size of a pumpkin.

Ratchet grimaced, shoving away his mug of syrupy green coffee. Gingerly, he picked up a fork and scraped a speck of crusty egg off a prong. "Incantus Gothmog thought she was silly too," he mumbled, keeping his eyes glued to the dirty floor, "but she hammered him and his army of dorfmorons and demons."

Glumweedy snorted, giving him the skunk eye. "Ratchet, you muppet, if you had only an egg cup full of guts."

The other wizard gulped, cowering on his stool.

"There's no risk in this for you, man, and you got y' gold, remember?" Glumweedy snapped his fingers. He wanted to order a second kebab. "Listen, just be in Twice Brewed on Sunday. I'm planning to rally a bit of support."

The wizard looked at him quizzically, as if sizing him up for a padded cell. He rested his trembling fists on the table, trying not to smear a splodge of jam in the shape of a Wellington boot. "But Mr Glumweedy, Sir," he stammered, "the wizards of Twice Brewed will never get rid of The Wishing Shelf. Where will they buy magic books from? Hedes Spine went bust."

"Let's just say, The Wishing Shelf has a monster of a problem," Glumweedy chuckled, "or should I say, a problem of a monster."

Looking edgy, Ratchet chewed on his thumb. "A monster? But how...?"

The fat wizard tapped the side of his nose. "Secret," he mocked him, "but if the Quill 'n' Scroll gets wind of it, the wizards in this town will be begging me to turf Brady out."

A whiskery hag in a grimy pink apron waddled over. She had 'dinosaur crushing' thighs and a wart the size of a Maltese on her left eyelid. "What is it!?" she spat. "I'm busy."

"A kebab, my angel, go easy on the ketchup, lots and lots of mustard and a good dollop of chilli." He leered at her. "I like it spicy!"

Puckering up her mouth like a cat's bottom, the hag rolled her eyes and grunted. Then she hobbled over to the kitchen. "Kebab, hot 'n' spicy," she hollered, "for the fat geezer in the corner."

Fester chuckled and shot a wink at the wizard next to him. "I think I'm in there."

Ratchet shifted his eyes to the droopy wand flashing in the window. It was creepy how sharp Glumweedy's radar was.

"We need a super-cunning plan," declared Felicity, snatching up a poker and duelling a blackened log. A shower of sparks flew up and a rug by her feet growled and scampered away in disgust.

Al, who was sprawled on the sofa, sucked in his cheeks and scratched his mop of curls. Felicity's fingers itched to comb it. "Yep," he agreed, "we do." There was a long silence. "Can we trick him?"

"Oh, yes."

"Jolly good." A much longer silence followed and Felicity wondered if she should kick him. "I'd think a lot better if I had..."

"A whopping big mug of tea?" suggested Felicity, her shoulders drooping.

Slapping a cushion, the imp jumped up. "You got it, baby doll."

Why did he keep calling her that? Had he been watching old Frank Sinatra films? On his t-shirt a black kettle was saying to a black cauldron,

WHAT DID YOU JUST CALL ME!?

Dragging her feet, she followed him over to the kitchen. She had a sinking feeling asking Al for help was as sensible as patting a drooling dorfmoron. She watched him fill up the kettle and lug it over to the stove.

"Just conjure up a cup of tea," she suggested, a little irritably.

Al looked at her, aghast. "Magic is sort of okay, but a teabag..."

Rubbing her eyes and wishing her staff worked a bit harder, she plonked her bum on a wonky stool. She often wondered why every stool in The Wishing Shelf was wonky. Were they just really old or were they all from a wonky stool shop?

Well, she had asked the handyman to fix them so maybe in the next few days...

She grunted. Quicker to employ a slug to crawl over to IKEA, buy twenty new stools, then drag them over to the shop, stopping for a coffee and a jammy doughnut.

Over on the stove squatted a bubbling pot. It hiccupped, making Felicity jump. "Fancy a bowl of rat and frog casserole?" it quizzed her.

"Er, no thanks."

"Rabbit, then, and a dash of wart puss?"

"Tempting, but no."

"Yukocot and spider legs?"

"No, honestly, just wolfed a packet of prawn cocktail crisps."

Grunting, it banged down its rusty lid. In The Wishing Shelf, even pots and pans had feelings.

"We still need a sneaky plan," Felicity persisted. "How can I get hundreds of wizards and hags to support me?"

The imp glared at her, patting his foot on the floor. "Just wizards and hags?" he pouted.

"Oops, sorry." She smiled apologetically. "Imps can sign it too I, er - think. I'll ask Kitta."

Grabbing up a stripy green and blue mug, the imp crossed over to Felicity and shoved it in her hands.

"Today, you can choose the tea you want."

"Brilliant."

"Skunk and bongeroo worm droppings or pond scum?"

"Hmm, difficult."

The imp nodded, gravely, as if they were discussing politics or starving people in Africa. "Yes, it is. Depends on your mood. The skunk and bongeroo worm droppings is super yummy but a bit spicy. It can creep up on you and fill you with wind." He swelled up his chest, looking proud. "I can empty a room in under ten seconds."

Felicity cringed. "Pond scum will do the job."

He went to fetch a teabag.

"I know," Al called over to her, "we could have him killed."

"What!?"

"Glumweedy. Shove him off a cliff or blow up his carpet. I know a chap..."

"In my book, murder is a big no-no."

The imp tutted, pouring the tea as if it was the water of life. "How can I help you if you keep poo-pooing all my best plans."

Felicity put her head in her hands.

"What if we just hurt him really, really badly. If he lost a leg or two. I know," he clapped his hands, "we could pull his teeth out."

"NO!"

"Not even a toe?"

Luckily, Felicity was stopped from throttling the imp with the kettle by the welcome sound of clomping boots in the shop.

She jumped to her feet. CUSTOMERS! "We can drink tea later," she told the distressed imp. "Come on, I may need a hand."

They rushed out of the kitchen and back to the front of the shop, but they were met not by a wizard or a witch, but what looked to be a family of hippos.

"Oooh, a shop," bawled a plump man. He had on horrible green shorts, sandals and a Bugs Bunny t-shirt.

"Oooh, a book," howled a woman. She was the size of a small bus and could only be the man's wife. That, or a sumo wrestler.

Felicity rolled her eyes. Trolls were bad, goblins terrible, BUT FAT TOURISTS!

Hands on hips, she glared over at the imp. "You lemon!" she exploded. "You left the door open."

But poor Al was too busy fending off a chubby boy who was patting him and trying to pick him up. "Look Ma, Pa," he was shouting, "a puppy. Can I keep him? Can I? Can I?"

This helped Felicity to feel only marginally better.

It took forever to get rid of them and only when the 'Witch Spotter's' book flapped her covers and yelled, "Kill 'em, boys", did they bolt for the exit.

But when they got there, the door swung open and a wizard in a green Mac strolled in, a gnome carrying a camera on his heels.

"Snap a shot of this lot," the wizard ordered, wagging a finger at the scarpering family.

The gnome sniggered and lifted up the camera. A bulb flashed, capturing three big bottoms, clambering to get through the door.

Felicity jumped to her feet in horror. They had just run out to Eternus!

Smirking, the wizard strolled over to Felicity and presented her with a dazzling smile. "So, you must be the new owner, Miss Brady," he gushed, a drop of spit hitting her cheek. She wiped it off.

He had a twitchy left eye and buckteeth even a vampire would be jealous of.

Squaring her shoulders, Felicity nodded. She felt rather proud.

"Barnaby Razz," he introduced himself, shaking her hand. It felt all limp and clammy. "I am a reporter on the Quill 'n' Scroll. I was hoping to have a quick chat."

Fantastic! A bit of free publicity. Feeling the proper hostess, she led him over to the sofa and instructed the imp to go pop the kettle on.

"A nice cup of tea." She stressed the word 'nice', crossing her fingers.

He skipped away looking way too happy.

The wizard flipped open a pad and, rather cheekily, rested his feet up on the table. "So, Felicity, the first girl to ever own The Wishing Shelf."

"I am?"

"Oh yes. Did nobody tell you? And a Brady too, not even a Falafel."

Felicity nodded. "Tantalus Falafel left me the shop in his will."

"Best of pals, hey?"

She did not even bat an eyelid. "He was like a dad to me," she deadpanned back.

"You must have lots of plans."

She nodded and began to tell him all the stuff she was hoping to do. Annoyingly, he did not seem to be writing any of it down.

"A lot to do, then," he interrupted her, just as she was describing her plans to invite Randolph P Plotinus for a book signing, "for a young girl."

She shrugged. "I guess."

"And on top of all that, you now control the door to all the magical lands."

"Yes, I suppose I do. But anybody can go through it. Free of charge," she added with a lopsided grin.

He scribbled in his pad. "How very kind of you."

Felicity scowled. She had only been joking.

The reporter smiled disarmingly. "Now, let's chat about this monster."

Felicity could almost feel her stomach filling with acid. "Huh!?"

Flamboyantly, Barnaby Razz flipped over a page in his pad. "Anonymous tip off, it seems. A letter by Imp Post. Says a lot of your customers seem to be going missing. Not a brilliant start, is it?"

"Huh?"

"I see," Felicity wished he'd stop scribbling, "so there's no truth in reports of," he glanced at the pad on his knee, "a Matilda Lemming popping in the shop to buy a book on poppodils and never popping back out." He emphasised all three 'pops'.

"Who?"

The wizard sighed, glancing over at the door. "Not very busy, is it?"

Wishing she had never agreed to this interview, Felicity shrugged, lamely. "We get the odd poor day," she mustered.

"I understand," the reporter simpered. Felicity had a feeling he did not 'understand' at all. "So, there's no monster? I can quote you?"

"No, there's not, and yes, you can." She crossed her fingers, hoping a blood-curdling roar would not suddenly fill The Wishing Shelf.

He nodded, scribbling furiously. He seemed satisfied. "And can you do magic?"

"Hey?"

"Well, if you can, no problem, but if you can't, well, a young girl with no, er, skills, running a magic bookshop..."

Felicity scowled.

The gnome snapped a shot of her.

Just then, the imp strolled in carrying a tray. "Goblin snot," he announced.

With a whimper, Felicity put her head in her hands.

The reporter smirked. "The Wishing Shelf really is going to the dogs."

"What's going to the dogs?"

Saucer-eyed, Felicity looked up. To her delight, Hickory had just stomped in the door, on his heels the family of hippos. They were being herded in the shop by Kitta. Bagel was helping too, pretending to be a sheep dog.

"So, there I was," began Hickory, "trying to buy a wonky stool..."

So, shops did sell wonky stools.

"...when in trots this lot." He waved his hand at the fat family.

Kitta shot Felicity a filthy look. "I wonder how they got to Eternus."

Felicity shrugged, her eyes wide. "I wonder."

"Oooh, I know, I know," howled the imp, his hand shooting for the roof.

Felicity's eyes shot daggers at him. Hanging was just too good.

Uncomfortably, she watched Hickory stroll over to The Clock by the Door. "England," he mumbled.

She stood up and resignedly helped them to shepherd the ashen-faced family out of the shop.

Messed up!

I met a reporter from the Quill 'n' Scroll and I told him, 'No, no monsters in The Wishing Shelf.' But I think there is. Met the handyman and he told me, very, very slowly, that there is a monster in here. The fool feeds him chunks of liver and milk every day. He's not a ruddy dog! Anyway, told the handyman to stop doing it, so maybe the monster will just go away. I just wonder if it, whatever IT is, is the monster that keeps waking me up every night.

I think he grabbed a witch called Matilda. But she's sort of annoying, always nattering on, so that's okay.

Oh, and I let a family of tourists go to Eternus. I bet they got a bit of a shock! Kitta blamed me. I told her the imp let them in, but no, all my fault. She is so annoying but Hickory thinks she is sweeter than a bag of 'pick 'n' mix'.

Maybe, she's put a spell on him. She is very good at them. How awful. Must tell Hickory.

My birthday tomorrow. I wonder if Mum will buy me lipstick and eyeliner. I want the ABBA CD too. Super Trooper is such a cool song.

Chapter 9

A Maggot in Snot Stew, Hags' Eyeballs in Goo

Elbowing open the door, Felicity stepped into the shop. Annoyingly, it was still dark. She tutted. It was the imp's job to top up the oil lamps but he was probably still in his cot dreaming of poodle and cactus tea.

She stumbled over to the desk, knocking over a stool and groping for the lamp. But just then, a shout rang through the shop.

"HAPPY BIRTHDAY!"

Felicity jumped in horror, stubbing her big toe, smacking her funny bone on a shelf and her left knee on the leg of the desk.

A glow now filled the shop fuelled by a hundred flickering oil lamps.

The Wishing Shelf looked to be packed to the bat-filled rafters. Dorothy, Fidget Moth, the imp and Pyjamas, his cat, Cuthbert the WANDD agent, the gargoyle Bogsnark, Hickory and Kitta, even Bartholomew Banks slumped in a gloomy corner.

"Flipping heck!" Felicity bawled, nursing her poorly knee. Then, on spotting Kitta, "I almost wet my knickers."

Clambering up on a stool, Fidget Moth held up a black baton.

"On three," he instructed the room.

But Hickory and Cuthbert had already begun to sing. With the rest of the room playing catch-up, Felicity had difficulty following all the words but it went something like this.

"Happy Birthday to you,
A maggot in snot stew,
You smell of smelly goblin paws,"

"They're hands!" yelled Banks from the back.

"And the stuff that they poo.

Happy Birthday to you,
Hag's eyeballs in goo,
A dorfmoron is super ugly,
But is no match for you."

Everybody clapped. Felicity smiled and vehemently wished a rottweiler would dash in, clamp his jaws on her foot and drag her from the shop.

"Speech!" bellowed Banks.

If Felicity's eyes had been the barrels of a shotgun, the goblin would be lying on his back bleeding profusely.

"Go on," Hickory egged her on, handing her a bowl of butterfly-yellow jelly.

She shrugged. For Hickory, anything.

"Er, thanks a lot for the balloons and the er, jelly." She tasted it and gagged.

"Nettle, bogey and banana," announced Al proudly.

The clanking of spoons in bowls abruptly stopped, but for Banks who was licking his bowl. "Blooming good grub," he declared.

"Today I am fifteen, so now I can legally do - nothing. Handy, as I'm not that busy. I got lots of presents, an ABBA CD from mum and dad," she held it up for everybody to see.

Lots of 'Wonderful!'s and 'Cool!'s filled the shop but Felicity had a feeling they all thought ABBA to be a sort of cooking oil.

"...and a yo-yo from Samuel, my baby brother. Oh, and my Aunty Imelda sent me a really old hourglass, I guess for my cookery class. Thanks for coming and don't forget to eat up all that yummy jelly!"

Then, she got the best present ever. Hickory hugged her. They stood and watched Professor Dement, who today had decided to be a jester. He had on baggy bloomers and a three-pronged hat, bells dangling off the tips. Hovering on a magic rug, he juggled yukocots, watering cans and even flower pots. They were particularly difficult for cacti grew in them.

Cuthbert popped a record on the old gramophone and soon The Wishing Shelf was filled with the sound of tapping feet. Felicity moseyed over to a balloon hooked on a lamp.

Interestingly, it kept morphing, from a barking baboon to a pooping parrot, from a pooping parrot to a grumbling goblin, from a grumbling goblin to a drooling dorfmoron ...

If only she had the magic in her to do that.

"Excellent speech," remarked Bogsnark. The gargoyle offered her his claw.

Shrugging, Felicity took it. He had helped Incantus Gothmog to trick her so she did not trust him. But in the end, he had killed the evil wizard so now she had sort of forgiven him.

"So, how's the spire?" she quizzed him, making chitter chat. "Did you get it back?"

"Yes." A smile chipped its way over his stony face. "I can see the River Cruor and on a good day, as far as Cauldron City."

"But Cauldron City is a dump."

"Yes. Yes, it is, but I can still see it."

Wrongfooted, Felicity looked over to where Cuthbert, Tanglemoth, Banks, Dorothy and Al were playing 'Pass the Parcel'. The goblin had been put in charge of the gramophone and under his watchful eye, Dorothy seemed to be doing awfully well.

Felicity tutted. No chins, no hairy spots and no black teeth; and the nurse still insisted she was a witch.

"Happy birthday." Kitta tapped her on the shoulder. "Here. For you." The charm maker handed her a gift.

Grinning, Felicity unwrapped it. A woolly jumper!

"Try it."

Felicity felt rather hot, but she shrugged and pulled on the jumper. To her astonishment, it got thinner and thinner till it was only a t-shirt.

"The warmer it is the thinner it is, the colder it is..."

"The thicker it is," finished Felicity, pulling it off. "Fantastic! Thanks."

Annoyingly pretty, Kitta had a pale, oval face and twinkling eyes. Today, she had on a chestnut dress and sandals on her tiny perfect feet. Recently, Felicity had begun to refer to her as 'Big Foot', just to annoy her.

"So, is it fun being the big boss of The Wishing Shelf?"

Felicity eyed her, sternly. "Maybe. If I had a tiny bit of help."

"But there's Al."

They looked over to the imp who had got his fingers tangled up in the parcel's ribbon.

"Just a tiny bit of help," repeated Felicity, sighing.

"Sorry," mumbled Kitta, looking embarrassed. "Been so busy sorting – things."

"Things!? What things?"

Patting her tummy, the witch glanced over at the clock. "In, say, fifty seconds I will tell you."

Felicity scowled, feeling annoyed. She had a feeling it was not going to be good news.

"How's school going?"

"Okay. I only got to go on the last day of term and I had to do a surprise maths test."

"Did it go well?"

Felicity chewed on her lip. "It was a very big surprise," she mustered dryly.

Tittering, Kitta pressed her hand to Felicity's cheek. Then, she left her there, walking over to Hickory and whispering in his ear.

The wizard clapped his hands. "Banks," he called over to the goblin. "Stop the music." He did and not surprisingly, Dorothy won, torn bits of the Quill 'n' Scroll littering her lap. "Just a few words," he began. "Felicity is now fifteen and is growing up to be a wonderful young lady." Grinning foolishly, Felicity felt she had just grown a foot taller. "She works hard to run The Wishing Shelf and go to school every day. Not easy and I am very proud of her. She's the kid sister I never had."

Felicity suddenly felt as tall as Banks. She did not want to be his 'kid sister'.

Now Kitta was talking. "...wonderful to see you all here and just to let you know Hickory and I plan to be wed in two weeks in Lupercus Castle."

What?!

"We hope to see you all there."

What?!

Everybody clapped.

WHAT?! Felicity felt crushed, tears of hurt stinging her eyes.

"For you." Banks handed her a gift.

"Oh, er, thanks." Her thoughts scattering like frightened birds. She was trying to look over his shoulder. Everybody seemed to be shaking hands, kissing Kitta and slapping Hickory on the back.

"Open it."

"In a sec."

"Go on."

Felicity gritted her teeth. "OKAY! OKAY!"

She ripped the paper off and discovered a tiny flying carpet. It hovered over her hand.

"If you remember, I blew up your old carpet."

She tossed him a stormy look. "I - remember - it - well," she seethed, filling each syllable. "But how will I fit on it or is it for a spider?"

The goblin chuckled and chanted,

> *"Missed the bus, in a tiz,*
> *Get MicroCarpet, the hi-tech whiz."*

In a flash, the carpet swelled up to full size.

"Cool, thanks." She glanced awkwardly at the goblin. "Why do you keep being so – nice?"

The goblin looked darkly at her. "Because, I am your father," he wheezed.

"What?!"

Banks chuckled, "Just kidding. Watched Star Wars yesterday. The old films, the classics, not the newer junk."

Felicity rolled her eyes. "So why?"

The goblin shrugged, "Soft spot for losers," he joked. "Look, Brady, you need to stop chasing after this Crowl-chap. It will never work."

"What?!"

"Do the maths. Hickory Crowl, a hundred and twenty-seven minus you, fifteen. I think that's ONE HUNDRED AND TWELVE! Plus he's soon going to be marrying a super-hot witch."

"Piffle!"

"What?!"

"Piffle!"

"What's a Piffle?"

"NOTHING!"

The goblin threw up his hands. "SO, WHY SAY IT?"

Glaring at him, Felicity lifted her nose, mumbled, "Lunatic," and stormed off.

Later on, when everybody had left, Felicity started the long job of tidying up. She popped all the balloons, dropped the leftover jelly (that being most of it) in the bin and scooped up the torn scraps of the Quill 'n' Scroll. In the corner of her eye, she spotted the word, 'MONSTER'. Nervously, she unscrunched the newspaper and jumped up on the desk.

A MONSTER OF A PROBLEM FOR THE WISHING SHELF STAFF
by Barnaby Razz

THE WISHING SHELF, the only magical bookshop in Twice Brewed, is in crisis. Over the last week, a witch and two wizards who were shopping there have vanished.

Felicity Brady, 14, the new owner of the shop, is reported to be befuddled by the recent events but, in her words, 'plans to do nothing'.

Mayor Glumweedy, 126, in an exclusive interview for the Quill 'n' Scroll, told us that if The Wishing Shelf had been left to a fellow wizard or even a witch, the monster could easily have been captured.

'The problem is, this Brady-girl can not do any magic, so there's no way she can stop a monster. And to add insult to injury, she now controls the only door to all the magic lands. Remember, she's from England and so was Incantus Gothmog. For all we know, the old tyrant was her dad.'

Fester Glumweedy, who also owns 'Stuff Y' Pets', is planning to take over the shop.

'Who needs books?' he asks. 'But we all need to stuff a pet. If you agree, pop in my shop and sign my scroll. If you do, we will stuff a fish for free.'

A goblin by the name of Bartholomew Banks, who wished to stay anonymous, told this paper, 'Felicity is doing a fantastic job. If I was not on the run for murder, kidnapping, battery, theft of the King of Mangbaloo's crown, pub brawling, hamster trapping, graffiti, spying, piracy, holding up a bank and littering a public footpath, I would gladly support her and sign her scroll.'

In the coming weeks, The Wishing Shelf's fate will be decided. Will it be a magic bookshop, a monster prowling the corridors, or a taxidermist, where no pet is too big or too small to stuff?

NEXT WEEK
Felicity Brady's love for a goblin! Exclusively in the Quill 'n' Scroll.

Felicity blew out her cheeks. "Oh boy!"

Chapter 10

Stepladders, Vipers and Chomping Chops

 "AL, SIT!"

Blowing a raspberry, the petulant imp dragged his feet over to the sofa and plonked his bottom on it. "If I was a dog," he carped, "I'd sleep in a kennel, chew on a bone and drool."

"YOU DO DROOL," retorted Felicity. She narrowed her eyes, shushing him. She only wished she could shush his t-shirt.

I often wonder...
'Why is that boomerang getting bigger?'
...and then it hits me.

"Okay, listen up boys and girls." Her fist thudded the top of the desk and everybody looked up. "We need every wizard and witch to sign the scrolls. Tell them how fantastic The Wishing Shelf is, how dust-free it is, that we plan to do lots of book signings and that Felicity, that's me, is doing a wonderful job."

The imp's hand popped up. "Can we bribe them?"

"No."

"Punch them in the chops?"

"No." Felicity rubbed her eyes.

"Grab a hostage?"

"No, no, no, no," the imp's hand stayed up, "and no, DO NOT pop the kettle on."

"Okay! Okay!," pouted the imp, his lower lip trembling. He nudged Fidget Moth. "Kettle! Ace idea."

"What is it, then?" Felicity barked. It was bound to be stupid.

"Can a yoblin or an impster sign it?"

Felicity scowled. She always felt a bit wrongfooted when he was sensible. "Er, I think you can ask anybody." She looked over to Kitta who nodded.

"If they've got teeth, they can sign."

Felicity scowled. What had teeth got to do with it!?

Recently, she had been a bit upset with Kitta and Hickory. They had not seemed very interested in her problems or helping her but seemed happy to spend hours and hours sitting in corners and whispering. Planning the wedding, she now guessed.

"And just keep in mind, whoever gets the most wizards..."

"Racist," shouted Al.

"...OR imps, to sign the scroll will get a prize." She lifted up a small box. "A packet of the finest Darjeeling tea." Her dad had told her to always try a bit of bribery to egg on the troops.

"Whoopee!" Al jumped to his feet, dashed over to the door and vanished.

"That got rid of him," murmured Fidget.

Tanglemoth, the spindlysloth sitting next to him on the sofa, chuckled.

Felicity dug in her Bart Simpson pencil tin and tossed everybody a pen. Holding his up to the window, Hickory asked, "Why do I need this?"

Felicity rested her balled-up fists on her hips. "Pen! Sign! Pen! Sign!"

"Yes," Hickory nodded slowly, "and...?"

Owning a bookshop was very stressful, Felicity decided. "Let's just go. And Hickory, bring the pen."

"Okay boys," bellowed Glumweedy, "listen up! I need every wizard and witch we can strong-arm to sign the scrolls. Remember to tell them how rubbish The Wishing Shelf is and that Felicity Brady, that silly girl, is doing a shockingly bad job."

A hand with a gold ring on the thumb shot up. "Mayor Glumweedy, if they still say no, can we bribe them?"

"A bit of a sweetener, hey." The wizard nodded. "Good thinking, Elark."

"Can we punch 'em too?"

"The harder the better."

"Grab a hostage?"

Putting on his hat, Glumweedy clapped his hands in glee. "Elark, you need therapy, but I think you'll go a long way. Let's go, boys."

Sniggering and jeering, the gang of wizards trooped out of The Droopy Wand Café.

Glumweedy strutted after them, his mind full of plans for The Wishing Shelf. But uttermost in his mind was his plan for the bookshop door; his secret plan. If magical folk were so keen to travel to all the different lands, so be it, no problem, but they'd be paying him to do it.

Fester Glumweedy, soon to be the new owner of The Wishing Shelf, was planning to put a toll booth on the bookshop door!

Felicity stood in the square, her hands folded over her scroll. Surrounded by twisted old shops, lollipop trees and gobstopper ferns, she had never seen so many wizards and hags. Not in The Wishing Shelf anyway. Mostly, they stood in front of shabby stalls, haggling over the cost of a yukocot or a flying carpet. She spotted a skinny wizard fling open his cloak to show a gang of giggling hags the vials of venom hanging in the lining. A bronze statue of a wizard crowned the very centre of the square. To Felicity's surprise, he whipped off his hat and wiped bird poo off the rim.

"If I ever catch that blooming wigglefinch," she heard him mutter.

The sky threatened rain and everybody seemed to be in a rush. How was she going to stop any of them?

The rest of her gang of helpers looked to be having problems too, except for Al, who was dashing from wizard to wizard in his bid to win the Darjeeling tea.

Clenching her teeth, she hopped in front of a witch. "Can I..."

"No," she huffed, "I sponsored a yoblin yesterday, I don't want to talk about God and I'm already in the AA." She marched off.

Felicity looked on in amazement. They had the AA in Eternus!?

"Felicity, this is a doddle," yodelled Al, scampering past her.

She watched a hag bite the imp's scroll. So that was why they did not need a pen. She remembered Grand Duke Franz Figglewick. Not just a vampire thing, then.

Okay, the big guns were coming out. She was gonna have to flirt.

"Can I stop you," she smiled sweetly at a little old wizard, "just for a sec?"

The wizard, who looked to be over a thousand years old, halted. Felicity concentrated on not concentrating on the wart on the tip of his crooked hooter. She wondered if he'd put fertilizer on it.

"My name is Felicity Brady," she shouted. He was bound to be deaf. "Perhaps you know me? I own a bookshop called The Wishing Shelf."

"No. Why you shouting, girl? Do I look like an oozing slug bat?"

"Erm, no," Felicity did not really get it. "The thing is, Fester Glumweedy, fat chap, big bum, is trying to hoodwink (she had looked the word up and decided it was excellent) my bookshop. So I need to get as many wizards and hags as I can to sign my scroll. Then, I can stop him."

"Glumweedy!?" The wizard sucked on his gums. "He's the mayor."

"Is he?" Felicity thought he had just been trying to impress her.

The wizard snorted. "He told me, if I voted for him, I'd get a new carpet pass. He's full of..."

"Got a hundred and two," yelled Al, cartwheeling past them.

The old wizard fumbled in his cloak and to Felicity's disgust pulled a set of false teeth out of his pocket. "Lost 'em ten years ago," he told her, snapping them on her scroll, "in a pub brawl."

Felicity looked at the bite mark in delight. "Thanks very, very much," she exploded, planting a kiss on his pot-marked cheek.

The wizard blushed. "Follow me." He took her by the arm. "Just off to play Stepladders and Vipers. There'll be lots of my old pals there who'll gladly sign your scroll. Glumweedy promised them a carpet pass too."

He led her over to a shadowy corner and then down a murky alleyway. Chock-full of foreboding, Felicity followed the wizard to the very end and to the most creepy-looking house you, or I, or even a ghost, can think of; the sort of place poltergeists happily go on holiday. Dressed in a sombre jacket of blackened wood and sharpened corners, Felicity felt as if the house was snarling at her, daring her to walk up the cracked steps. Wherever she looked, elderly crooked trees and old tombs stood on sentry duty. Most of the tombs had toppled over as if they had wriggled free, scared of what lay under them.

"Charming" muttered Felicity.

A bit of driftwood had been nailed to the door. On it, in big red letters, 'Ye Olde Banshee pub'. Felicity cringed, wondering if it was written in blood.

Banks' old haunt, she remembered. She just hoped the goblin was not in there.

With feet of lead, Felicity trailed the wizard up the steps and in the (Surprise! Surprise!) creaky door. In fact, it kept on creaking even after it had shut.

"Coo-ee! It's me-ee!"

Banks! The goblin ambled over with a tankard of smoking Grogbog clutched in his hand. He clapped her on the back.

"Fancy a beer, kid?"

Felicity tossed him a disapproving look. "It's illegal for kids to drink beer."

The goblin chuckled. "Yes, it is, but it's really, really funny."

Trying to pretend Banks did not exist, Felicity strolled over to the bar, the floor under her feet creaking like a room full of OAP's doing jumping jacks. Gnarled wizards hid in corners and spiders, so big they guzzled from thimble-sized tankards, hung in the rafters.

A witch stood by the bar, her hand draped over a cask of Daddy Long Legs beer. She had on a grey gypsy shawl and a tatty dress splashed all over with faded red dots.

The landlady, Felicity guessed.

The witch stared at her, transfixed. "Imelda Brady?" she mouthed.

"Er, no. Felicity. Imelda is my..."

"I spotted that nasty report in the Quill 'n' Scroll." The goblin had followed her over.

"Try not to talk to that reporter. He's a slimy old rascal, that Barnaby Razz. Sell his mum for a good story."

Felicity felt her jaw harden. "But you spilt y' guts to that 'slimy, old rascal' too."

"Hey," Banks held up his hands, spilling Grogbog on the floor, "just trying to help."

"Help! HELP! I'd rather get a reference of Hannibal Lecter." She stepped up to him. "How many laws did you break?"

The goblin started to count the fingers on his left hand.

"Oh, forget it."

"Fancy a bag of crisps, then?"

"What!?"

"They do salted, bacon, beetroot and smelly troll's underpants."

Shrugging him off, she chased after the old wizard who had led her there. She had just spotted him slipping out of a door at the back of the pub. It led her into a room full of even older wizards. They were huddled by the far wall and on the wall a grid had been drawn. Ladders hung linking a number of the boxes and, to her horror, there were lots of snakes.

Felicity had a terrible feeling this was Stepladders and Vipers.

"Wonna play?" the wizard asked her, on finding him. But he was looking past her.

She looked over her shoulder and there was Banks.

The goblin shrugged. "Okay, Istor, why not?"

Istor fixed his hand to the shoulder of a witch. "This is my Counter."

Felicity already guessed what was coming. Banks grinned at her. "And Brady here will do for me."

"What shall we bet?" Istor quizzed him.

"I got a sack of..."

But Felicity butted in. "If we win you get all your old pals to sign my scroll."

"And if I win?"

"Oh, er..."

The goblin dropped a sack on the floor. It clinked. "You get this."

Felicity looked quizzically at the goblin. Why did he keep on helping her? Did he still fancy her? Reluctantly, she flashed him a smile.

She followed the witch over to the wall and they stood next to the box marked 'START'. Looking up, Felicity could see there was a narrow shelf under each row, she guessed to walk on.

"Roll to go first?" suggested Banks.

Istor nodded and rolled a '2'. Grinning, the goblin shook his fist and rolled a '6'. Excellent! They got to go first. The old wizards crowded closer to the wall as Banks shook and rolled the dice.

A '3'.

Felicity walked three steps and climbed a ladder to square twenty-four. She grinned down at the goblin and showed him a 'thumbs up'.

But Istor then rolled a '6'. He got a second roll. A '4'. The witch swaggered over to square ten looking annoyingly smug.

Banks blew on his fist and rolled his dice.

A '1'.

"Nuts!" he mumbled.

Felicity walked a step, all her optimism sinking into her shoes.

But then disaster really struck as the wizard threw a '2' and the grinning witch got to climb all the way up to thirty-three.

Only seven steps to the finish!

The goblin rolled a '4' and thankfully she climbed up to square thirty-five. A viper in the very next box snapped at her feet.

Istor, now looking a tad pasty, rolled his dice. To Felicity, it seemed to skip and bounce forever as if hunting for a particular number. She glanced over at Banks. He had shut his eyes and he looked to be mumbling. Then it hit the wall and finally stopped on '3'.

Glumly, the witch walked past her. Felicity patted her on the back. "Tough luck," she muttered, trying to smother her delight.

As the witch stepped on the square, the snake swallowed her up. Felicity watched in disgust as a witch-shaped bulge slid down the viper's wriggling body. Finally, looking all green and sticky, she tumbled out onto square eighteen.

Casually, Banks rolled a '5' and Felicity skipped over to the finish. In a flash, she was standing next to the smirking goblin.

Istor did not seem too bothered and shook the goblin's and Felicity's hands. He turned to the other wizards. "Okay boys…"

Boys! Maybe a hundred and fifty years ago.

"…Felicity here is going to tell you why it is so important you sign her scroll."

"Cheat," Felicity mumbled to the goblin.

"ME! NO! NEVER! Now, get up on a table," he urged her.

"Why? No. You do it."

"All of this lot will probably be deaf. They will hear you better up there."

Sighing, Felicity did as she was told.

"The Wishing Shelf is a wonderful bookshop," she began, "every book has a tale to tell and every shelf is full of secrets to be discovered. If Fester Glumweedy, and remember, that's the chap who forgot to buy any of you a carpet pass, gets his hands on my shop, he will throw the history of Eternus, your history, in a big yellow skip. Also, my imp brews a wonderful cuppa and we now offer HobNobs and monster Kit-Kats."

"Brilliant!" called Banks.

"Crikey," mumbled Istor, standing just next to him. "When you wind her up, she never stops."

Yelling and hammering, clattering spoons on beer cans, the elderly wizards crowded in on her to sign her scroll. All of a sudden, there were snapping false teeth everywhere.

Climbing off the table, she grinned over at the goblin. But to her surprise, he appeared to be scowling. She tutted. Never happy.

"Wonderful, wonderful speech!" Twisting her head, Felicity spotted Fester Glumweedy in the crowd. He walked over to her.

"Thanks," she muttered.

The wizard shrugged. "Too good for me. I offer my hand in defeat."

Fantastic!

Trying not to look too smug, Felicity grasped Glumweedy's hand. For a split second, in the corner of her eye, she spotted Banks.

Oddly, he seemed to be trying to get to her, elbowing the old wizards out of his way.

KAPOW!

A bomb seemed to explode in her mind and she grabbed for her eyes, yelping in agony.

Thankfully, the throbbing quickly subsided as if she had swallowed the world's strongest Aspirin and she slowly lowered her hands.

Felicity's chin hit her chest and she felt her knees buckling under her. To her horror she seemed to be on a ship and the ship seemed to be sinking.

"Now I'm in the poo," she muttered.

Chapter 11

Por Larranga and a Pinch of Snuff

A man in a yellow lifebelt shoved by her, knocking her to the deck. For a split second he hesitated but terror clouded his eyes and he dashed off. "Sorry," he called belatedly over his shoulder.

Felicity scrambled to her feet. "Moron," she mumbled, nursing her elbow.

Surprisingly, she had on a long flowery dress and under it - she peeked - FRILLY BLOOMERS! A bonnet crowned her curls and flimsy slippers hid her feet. She prodded her top lip with her tongue and tasted lipstick.

Gingerly, the deck being waterlogged, she walked over to a metal railing lined with lifebuoys. A gigantic funnel loomed over her, lit up by the moon, and next to a porthole, a small orchestra of violins and a lonely cello thumbed a playful melody.

Most of the passengers milling the deck looked to be in a daze. Oddly, they had on pyjamas, hats and boots, shivering in bright yellow lifevests. They needed to be told what to do but apparently nobody wanted the job.

Peering over the rail, she discovered to her horror that the giant ship was already half under water. A rocket flashed, exposing a lifeboat half full of weeping girls and silent mums. Wheels creaked and men grunted as they were lowered down to the glassy water.

"Put this on, lass," a uniformed man shoved a lifevest in her hand, "and get to a boat."

Felicity gripped hold of his sleeve. "What ship is this?" she bleated. "Where am I?"

But he seemed to be in an awful hurry. Pulling free, he dashed off, flinging vests to the other frightened passengers.

Slipping the yellow vest on, Felicity spotted a word embossed on the front and got the biggest shock of her life. She seemed to be finding it difficult to focus her eyes. She grabbed for the rail, TITANIC embedded in her mind.

Did Fester Glumweedy send her here? But why? And how did he do it?

Felicity felt her feet slipping, the ship tilting slowly over, whimpering in agony. Her knuckles turned white as she gripped the metal bar. She had to keep her feet dry and find room on a lifeboat. But where to go? Twenty feet away water gurgled and splashed over the deck. Probably away from the rising water, she guessed. She remembered, in the film, everybody had frozen to death.

Further up the deck, she spotted a portly man wearing a top hat and curly whiskers. Hand over hand, she struggled over to him. "Can you help me?" she panted. "I need to get off this ship. I need to find a lifeboat."

Smirking, the man chewed off the tip of a cigar and lit it with a match. "Cuban," he informed her, blowing a wonky smoke ring. "They call it the Por Larranga. Enveloped in a fine cedar leaf. Cost me twenty shillings." He offered it to her. "Try a puff."

Felicity goggled at him. "No, thank you. Er, the ship's sinking..."

"Yes, my girl, it is. Mr William B Greenfield, by the way. I do enjoy a good pipe too and a pinch of snuff. Sadly, I left my pipe in the cabin and my snuff's a smidgen too damp. So, a cigar it is."

Bonkers!

Felicity pulled off her lifevest and stuffed it in the man's hand. "Put it on," she ordered him. "I think it knots at the front."

Ripping off her hat and the slippers, she left him standing there, shaking his head. "I think I shall go and play cards with Alfred and Henry," he announced, stubbornly.

Felicity had to find a way off this doomed ship. If only she had the woolly jumper Kitta had given to her. It was absolutely freezing.

Suddenly the sound of twisting metal punished her ears and she looked up to see the funnel slowly toppling over. "Watch it," she yelled to a bonneted lady, up to her knees in swirling water. Too late. The funnel landed in the water with a splash, crushing her.

Unblinking, Felicity looked on in horror, her feet rooted to the deck of the ship.

Over to her left stood a crowd of passengers, shouting and yelling, trying to get off the Titanic. A man in a uniform, holding a pistol, held them back. "Children first, gentlemen," he hollered.

Felicity knew she had to forget the poor lady. She had to get off the ship.

Running over, she jostled her way through the angry mob. A lady in a ball gown trod on her foot and a boy slapped her in the left eye, but Felicity kept on going, pushing and shoving, elbowing her way to the front. Finally, she got there, but to her horror the lifeboat had already left.

"But there's still lots of room," she shouted indignantly at the man.

He ignored her.

"Hey!" She grabbed for his sleeve.

Like lightning, he lowered his pistol, cocking it in her face. "Back away," he commanded her, his words shaking in time with his hand.

"Okay, okay," whimpered Felicity, the tip of the barrel tickling her nose.

The angry spark in his eyes softened and in disgust, he tossed the pistol away. "Sorry," he mumbled. "Try over on the port side. There may still be boats."

"Okay."

"But hurry," he urged her, nudging her in the square of her back.

Felicity tripped and scrambled her way over the slippery deck. Steeper and steeper, the ship tilted over and Felicity had to grab hold of ladders and the rim of a porthole to stop herself from hurtling off the ship. Everywhere, men helter-skeltered over the shiny deck, yelling in panic and crying for help.

Scrambling over a fallen mast, Felicity finally got to the port side. But to her horror the lifeboats had vanished, a winch and a dangling rope the only clue to where they had vanished to.

"Did all the boats go?" she shouted to the panicking passengers.

They ignored her but for a scruffy-looking lady clinging to the rail. "They left us," she whimpered. "The posh lot left us here." Turning her back on Felicity, she jumped, her cry filling the bitterly cold night.

A deep growl rumbled in the stomach of the Titanic and the lights blinked off, drowning the ship in a black cloak. Felicity stood there, only a tiny whimper invading her terror.

The twinkling stars helped Felicity to spot the small boy wedged under the ladder. She crept over and nestled in next to him.

"Where's your mum?" she asked him kindly. His hands were shaking. On impulse, she covered them in her own.

"I lost her," he snivelled, his words quivering. He had on stripy pyjamas and boots on his feet. He looked to be seven or so. "Can you help me to find her?"

"Okay," she promised him, squeezing his hand. "Soon. If I can."

The Titanic seemed to be almost vertical now, only the ladder stopping them from sliding away, and soon the whole ship would be submerged and they would be at the mercy of the freezing water. Felicity remembered in the film, Jack had been killed by hypothermia.

There had been no room on the raft for him and Rose. How selfish was that? A tremor rocked the ship, masking the sound of frothing water.

Only seconds to go.

She remembered the boy wedged in next to her. "I'm Felicity."

"B-B-Benjamin," he stuttered back.

"So," Felicity racked her brains; it was very difficult to think of things to say sitting on the sinking Titanic, "do you enjoy watching TV?"

"What's a TV?"

"Oh, right," she mustered a tiny grin, "sorry, but when you get to forty..." the words lodged painfully in her throat. No 'Muffin the Mule' or 'Bill and Ben the Flowerpot Men' for poor Benjamin.

The swirling water rushed over her bare feet and legs, surging up her body and filling her screaming mouth. It was agony, a thousand pins being jabbed all over her skin. Grimly, she held on to Benjamin's hand and she felt his tiny fingers squeezing hers.

Anger filled her mind. Anger at Glumweedy; that he now had his hands on

The Wishing Shelf. Anger at Hickory, Kitta, Fidget, Al, all of them, for not properly helping her to stop him.

Suddenly, Felicity felt her stomach being yanked as if she'd been hooked on a fishing line and she felt the boy's tiny fingers slipping away. A split second later, oxygen filled her lungs and the freezing water stopped stabbing her skin.

Slowly, she lifted her eyelids, half expecting to be on a cloud, tiny butterfly wings flapping on her back. But to her utter astonishment, she seemed to be standing in a large green tent.

"Well, this is much better," she mumbled.

Chapter 12

A Walk in the Park

"Relax, Captain. Grab a pew. Brandy? Rum? No? Good lad. You lot drink too much anyway. Wonderful news. We go over 'the top' in the morning. 6am." He chuckled, twisting his moustache. "When I say we, I mean you, you and your men. Lucky blighters. I need to stay here. I volunteered you, by the way. You get to carry the flag. For England and all that." He waved a hand at Felicity. "No, no, you can thank me when you get back. Have a butchers at this map. The Hun is here, dug in on the ridge, been up there over a year, only way to get to them is to go in the front door. Sappers been tunnelling for over a month. Plan is to stick a bomb under them, blow it, then over you go. Billy Biggins will be on your flank, good chap, I play bridge with his dad, general in the Boer War. Sadly, he missed this party. Lost his leg to a cannon. We plan to shell them good and proper too. The lot of them will probably be in shock, surrender or run off. A walk in the park for your lads, hey?"

Felicity looked at him blankly. Was he talking to her?

She was in a green canvas tent. The old man talking to her had on a uniform and so, it seemed, did she. Her feet felt cramped in tall, black boots and her skin itched under a woolly tunic. She was still freezing, but thankfully it was not as cold as being on the sinking Titanic. She had on a metal helmet and a rifle was slung over her shoulder.

She flexed her fingers. Only a moment ago she had been holding a small boy's hand. Poor Benjamin. She hoped he had survived.

"Chat to your men, captain, check gasmasks and bayonets. Bacon and jam for every man when they get back, and a day's rest. Keep low and watch for snipers. How's the trench foot?"

Felicity looked at her feet. She had no idea what trench foot was. He kept calling her a captain but did he not see that she was a fifteen-year-old girl? She was not even in the scouts.

"That bad, hey? Try a drop of whale oil. Do the trick. Okay, that's all, chop, chop. Remember, the Battle for the Somme may end the war."

He saluted her and she sort of waved feebly back.

Stumbling out of the tent, she was met by a gangly man, his legs caked in mud. "What did he say, Sir? We going over the top?"

"Yes, I think so." She took off the helmet. It felt so heavy. "In the morning."

The man's shoulders drooped. "Better get back and tell the rest of the lads, eh?"

Felicity nodded.

He set off. "Sir," he called over his shoulder, "better pop your tin potty back on. Lots of snipers, yeah."

Shoving the helmet on her head, she reluctantly followed him.

The night was dark, as if the moon had run away in disgust, and it was snowing in big, fat lumps. They seemed to be in the country. A flash of light, a gun Felicity guessed, lit up the sky for a second, showing her a forest of blackened trees. There were blisters on her feet and they burned as she staggered in mud up to her knees. A pony struggled by dragging a wagon. To her horror, it was full of injured men crying and whimpering. She was in a world of rattling guns, whiz-bangs and barbed wire.

They trudged on, Felicity keeping her hands hidden in the pockets of her trench coat. The rifle kept nudging her, reminding her of where Glumweedy had sent her.

To war.

"Is that you, Spink?"

"Nah, it's bleeding Santa. Lower your rifle, dimwit." Following Spink, Felicity climbed down into a trench. "Open your lugs, lads. The captain here has a wonderful job for us to do."

Perhaps twenty scruffy men were crouched in the ditch. Swimming in mud, they were scoffing corned beef out of battered tin trays. Forks clattering to a stop, they all looked up at her expectantly.

"Is it true, captain?" A young boy piped up, his eyes scared and bloodshot. "They sending us over?"

Felicity looked at him. How old? Eighteen? Nineteen? Perhaps a few years older than her? "Yes, soon. In the morning. After we shell them."

"The general reckons a walk in the park, eh, Sir?" offered up Spink. Had he been listening at the tent?

Felicity's lip felt dry. She remembered studying The Battle of the Somme in school. Nearly all the men had been shot. She nodded anyway.

"Yeah," she croaked. "A walk in the park."

Many of the men smiled but she spotted Spink did not. She had a feeling he knew the awful truth too.

Spink nudged the man next to him. "What did you get?"

"Sweets," he popped a yellow blob in his mouth, "lemon bonbons, I think and a letter from my dad." He looked up at Felicity who was resting her shoulder on the wall of the trench. "Will you read it to me, Captain? Never been much good with words. A bit fiddly, I find."

Felicity bent over and took the letter. Moving to stand next to a candle, she unfolded the damp paper.

To my son, Jacob, she read

Your mother and I hope this letter finds you well. She sends her love and told me to tell you she prays for you and your regiment every Sunday in church. Everyday, we read in the newspapers how gallantly you and your pals are fighting. It seems the Germans will surrender soon and the war will be over.

The men in the trench tittered at this.

"They got no idea," mumbled Spink dejectedly.

I talked to your old boss, Mr Crunch, at the mill yesterday. He told me there was plenty of work for you when you return, so stay safe, son. Oh, and the gate needs fixing. I will save that job for you too.

I do have some bad news. Your old chum, Bert Potts, got hit in the face by shrapnel. He's blind now but back with his family. I met his father in the pub and he told me he's not doing too well. He's missing all his chums over in France. When you get back, you must visit him.

Your sister Kitty has met a chap. Works in the hospital. A doctor. She is very keen. And Granny's dog got shot by a farmer.

Enjoy the lemon bonbons and by the way, your mother is knitting socks for you. Will send soon.

Your proud father

"Cheers, Sir." Jacob slipped the letter in his tunic pocket. "Old Bert, good lad, played keeper for the pub." He chuckled. "Let in so many goals, I thought he was blind anyway. What did you get, Spink?"

Spink was busy oiling his rifle. "A letter from my mum, my granny, my sister Clara and my girl, Polly. I think even the dog put paw to paper. But nobody sent me any socks. My foot's killing me."

Trench foot, thought Felicity. She remembered her dad had always told her to keep her feet dry and warm. "Try whale oil," she suggested, remembering what the general had told her too.

Spink nodded. "Thanks, I will."

"You gonna read y' letters?" Jacob asked him.

"Nah, when I get back."

"But what if..."

Spink tossed a bully tin at him. "If the Hun shoots me, granny's bad knees, Clara's antics in the hay loft and Polly whining that she has nobody to go to the theatre with is not going to be of any interest to me. But if they miss me, I can enjoy them over a bacon roll and a pot of jam."

Perched on a rusty oil drum, Felicity listened to them natter on. Why had Glumweedy sent her here, to France, to a trench, a hundred or so angry Germans dying to shoot her? Reluctantly, she glanced at her watch. Not long now. She had been up all night, checking off the hours. Mostly the men let her be. Too busy chatting: food and the lack of it, girls and the lack of them. A Welsh chap had started to sing, 'Oh, Danny Boy', but the shells screaming overhead had stopped him. In the night, a general had hopped in the trench and told them what a very important job they were going to do. Felicity was an officer of sorts too. The men looked to her for support so she smiled at them, patted the odd shoulder and was generally no help at all.

A tremendous explosion shook the trench. Felicity fell to her knees, muddy water drenching her body. Spink helped her up.

"That's the signal, captain," Spink informed her cheerfully. "The Sappers did the job. Us next."

Feeling shell-shocked, Felicity nodded. Panic started to creep up her body, turning her palms sweaty, clutching at her throat. The men were gathering at the foot of the ladders, ready to go up. Only a minute to go. Her lips felt dry and cracked. She had no words left in her but she mustered a 'Good luck' to the man next to her.

If Fester Glumweedy was watching her, she hoped he planned to whisk her off if a bullet had Felicity Brady etched on it.

"Y-You too, captain," a stuttered reply dripping with terror.

Back-patting.

Hugging.

Handshaking, then a whistle blow.

A grim-looking soldier clambered up the ladder. Clutching a rifle she had no idea how to work, Felicity clambered up after him.

Peering over the top, a labyrinth of muddy craters met Felicity's gaze. She felt her knees almost buckle as mortars spat, lost in the mist as if such terrible things needed to be hidden.

The man below her on the ladder slapped her leg. "Get going, Sir!" he yelled.

Scrambling up the last two rungs of the ladder, she set off, but her boots tripped over a body slumped in the mud and she tumbled to her knees. It was Jacob, his eyes glassy and staring. A hand grabbed her by the belt and yanked her to her feet.

It was Spink. "Keep up, Sir. Soon be back in the trench, then we can all grab a nap."

Felicity nodded, her eyes vacant, uncomprehending.

They rushed on, clattering guns spraying a lethal storm of metal at them. In front of her, next to her, all around, men fell in the mud, yells of agony filling her ears. Spink fell too. She collapsed next to him.

Shaking, his tunic torn and bloody, he grabbed for Felicity's hand. "I wish I had read my letters," he choked. "I miss my mum."

Felicity nodded. "Me too."

"And my foot's still killing me," he chuckled, spilling blood on his chin.

Gritting her teeth, Felicity squeezed his fingers. "I shall buy you new socks. I promise."

She felt a hammer blow in her stomach and she keeled over, her body covering Spink.

Over her head, the machine gun kept clattering away.

It seemed not to worry that all the soldiers had been killed.

Chapter 13

A Crazy Girl in the Office

 "FELICITY!"

She jumped up, knocking her elbow on a metal filing cabinet.

"Can you pop over to Sally's office and drop this on her desk?" A fat balding man handed her a stack of loose paper. "Oh, and tell her the meeting is at ten-thirty and not eleven." He squeezed her throbbing elbow. "Chop, chop. Soon be lunch."

Nodding dumbly, Felicity patted her stomach. But there was no bullet hole. She lifted up her shirt. And no blood. Not even a scar.

The man looked at her doubtfully, then waddled off looking important.

Now she seemed to be in a busy office. Everywhere, fingers tapped on plastic keys and coffee mugs hid in the corners of cluttered desks. A tall man in a polar-necked jumper stood photocopying and next to him a fax beeped and spilled its paper guts.

From the accents, they had to be American.

Felicity felt her shoulders slowly relax. Compared to being on the sinking Titanic and in a muddy trench being shot at by the German Army, a busy office seemed a bit on the Red Setter puppy side. Unless a rogue stapler or a hole punch suddenly attacked her.

Now, what to do with all this paper? She trudged over to a lift. Maybe Sally's office was on a different floor.

Up or down?

Up.

She pressed the button. A gold arrow over the doors twirled. It passed 94, 95, 96...

The door pinged open.

But Felicity did not step in. A horrible idea had just invaded her mind. No. NO WAY! No way Glumweedy had sent her there.

Tossing the paper on the carpeted floor, she marched over to the man by the photocopier.

"What day is it?" she barked, her hands all wet and clammy.

"Tuesday, all day," drawled back the man. He kicked the humming machine. "Can you fix this thing? I think there's no ink left."

Felicity ignored him. "No, no, what's the date?"

He scratched his chin. "The twelfth," Felicity relaxed, "no, hold on, I took the bus up to Boston two days ago, my pa's birthday, 87, so today's..."

"The eleventh," croaked Felicity, her nails digging in her palms.

The man nodded.

"So I guess your dad must be a Virgo."

"Yep, but he's not that picky. Lazy too, bit of a Gemini really. You know your star signs, don't you?"

But Felicity ignored him. She sprinted over to the window and there, rising up from the city of New York, stood a second silver tower.

Nervously, she scanned the sky. Nothing. She glanced over at a clock on the wall. 8.30. When had it happened? In the morning? She'd been in school. Did it matter? She had to get everybody out.

"Felicity, did you tell Sally?"

She looked blankly at the bald man. "What?"

"I told you to..."

"We need to go."

"Felicity, relax..."

"WE NEED TO GO!"

"Do you er, feel okay? It is hot in here." He took her hand but she shook him off.

Sprinting over to a desk, she jumped up on it, knocking over a pot of pens, scattering them on the carpet. "Listen up guys," she bellowed, "any second now, a plane is going to hit this tower. We need to get out of here."

Everybody in the office turned and looked at her. Then, as if they had all telepathically agreed that she was a lunatic, they went back to work.

"Felicity, get off the desk." It was the photocopy man. "I called Security..."

But over his left shoulder, Felicity had just spotted a black speck in the sky, moving fast. A bird maybe. Jumping off the desk, she elbowed past him and rushed over to the window. Fearing the worst, she squashed her nose up to the glass.

"There it is," she whispered. She turned to the man. "THERE IT IS!"

"Got a problem, Harry?" The security guard had now turned up.

Harry shrugged. "Felicity here seems to be having a bit of a meltdown."

"I am not," yelled Felicity. She waved her hand emphatically at the glass. "Do you see that plane? In a second it is going to hit this tower. We need to set off all the fire alarms."

The security man gawked at her, looking puzzled. "Is there a fire, then?"

"No! NO! Why can you not understand me? This tower is going to collapse."

She was getting nowhere. She dashed back over to the lifts, the men on her heels. There, just next to the doors, a red box on the wall, 'In the event of fire, smash the glass'. She lifted her elbow but a hand grabbed her shoulder and pulled her away.

"Get off me!"

"Now, now, just relax..."

"Er, Bill," Harry prodded the guard, "that plane is flying very low."

Felicity felt the guard's hand relax on her shoulder. Turning to look too, Felicity's jaw dropped to her chest. They had only seconds left.

"Grab my hand." Amazingly, Banks was standing next to her. "Grab it!"

"But I must try and help them…"

"Brady, there is nothing you or I can do."

"WHY!?"

She felt his hands cup hers. "BECAUSE THIS HAPPENED YEARS AGO!"

The floor quivered under her feet and the sound of twisting metal filled her ears. For a split second, she felt the skin on her cheeks melt and her eyebrows burn. Then a frosty wind blew over her and slowly, she forced open her eyes.

She seemed to be back in Twice Brewed, in the room in the pub. In front of her, still clutching her hand, stood Fester Glumweedy.

"Enjoy the history lesson?" he scoffed her.

"But - WHY!?" she snarled.

"Simple, I wanted to teach you how futile it is to battle destiny. The Titanic sinks, men in war get killed and mad terrorists do mad things. Nobody can stop it happening; it's stupid to try." He dragged her up to him. "The Wishing Shelf will very soon be Stuff Y' Pets. Undisputably so. It is a fact; it is written in the stars. You will not stop me; you can not stop me, so - why - bother - to - try."

Wrenching her hand away, her fingers grappled for his podgy neck. "YOU CRAZY MONSTER!" she yelled, rugby tackling him to the floor. "I'M GONNA KILL YOU! I'M GONNA KILL YOU!"

Chapter 14

Pots of Raspberry Fool

Perched on books, they giggle and chat,
A gang of monsters playing 'Pit a Pat Splat',
A trolley's wheeled out, pots of Raspberry Fool,
Elbows in ribs, slobbering drool,
Flippery feet to dip in the sea,
The tea cosy's off, they slurp on snot tea.

The glumsnappers plan a night on the town,
Ye Olde Banshee pub or the Spindlysloth Crown?
Cards and darts and bags of trolls' skin,
Crammed full of spiders to drop in girls' gin,
They skulk up the steps, silent and low,
As they live in The Wishing Shelf, but nobody knows.

Stubby chicken legs, flippers on the end,
A turnip snout with a bit of a bend,
Moon craters splattered on colander heads,
A black, woolly blanket to keep them cosy in bed,
In a puff of pink dust, the glumsnapper is there,
Speedy as a cheetah, tricky to snare.

Glumweedy's Devil

Giddy days of cheering judder to a stop,
Glumsnappers all cuffed, trussed up in knots,
Incantus Gothmog, a wizard to bow to,
Wielding Articulus, a book to cower to,
To battle they go, to fight wizards and imps,
But the enemy's strong, "Glumsnappers be wimps!"

A horror film of butchery, muskets and swords,
One lowly glumsnapper flees, bleeding and torn,
Hiding in swamps and farmers' haystacks,
Dodging the imps hunting in packs,
He creeps to the shop and slips in the door,
His breed now a myth, a part of folklore.

Sad days drag by, a shadow in the gloom,
Sipping on a cup of misery and doom,
Old stools, mad ghouls, books on Mangbaloo,
'How to Kill Dragons' and 'Cook Goblin Stew',
Like a flower on a tomb, a blob of ink on a page,
A stomach full of fury, hatred and rage.

Rows of black books, all murky and grim,
They sneer and jeer and snigger at him,
He hankers to sprawl on the rug in the shop,
Sit by the fire and drink tea from a pot,
But if he slips back in there, only a cage will he see,
The locks will be locked by a 'throw-away' key.

But a fat wizard finds him and shows him a plan,
The girl in the shop abhors all your clan,
Do you want to get even? Fill her with fear?
Then grab all the wizards who venture in here,
Rip 'em and kick 'em and cut 'em in two,
Show 'em what a woolly glumsnapper can do.

In a cobwebby corner he finds a 'Keep Fit' book,
Daily drills for the Schwarzenegger look,
Then he twists and he loops a magical string,
Crafting a net to trap his prey in,
With no carton of milk and no chunk of red liver,
The only thing left is the fish in the river.

Matilda Lemming, on her hands and knees,
Hunting for a book on poppodil seeds,
Then Fidget Moth, the next to be trapped
He scratched and he bit, he clawed and he snapped
Trussed up, tethered up, who's next for the chop?
The imp: spiky ears and a curly brown mop.

Chapter 15

Flubby Lubby Lub

Two days later, Felicity sat perched on a stool by the window, nursing a giant mug of cocoa and watching a crisp bag performing a waltz in the wind. A black cloud hung over Twice Brewed, threatening to wash the soot off the roofs and to scrub the streets. Spindlysloths mooched by and wizards on carpets dodged lampposts and crooked chimney pots.

That morning, she felt full of gloom and a tiny bit lost, her mind chock-a-block with thoughts of Spink and Jacob bleeding in the mud, Benjamin and his small fingers and poor Harry, the photocopy man.

Why them?

Why did the good guys get killed?

Before, she had always thought that if she had been on the Titanic or in a war or attacked by terrorists, she'd be the hero. But in fact she had saved nobody and had been killed too and now she felt utterly worthless.

Maybe Glumweedy was spot on; maybe running The Wishing Shelf was just too much for her. Lucy and Matilda, her pals in school, had already decided to go to Glodberry College next year. Maybe she should apply too; see a bit of her own world before trying to run a magic bookshop.

Suddenly a goblin jammed his nose up to the glass. Felicity jumped up, spilling cocoa on her jeans. A second later, the door flew open and Banks ambled in.

"Wotcha." He jumped up on the desk, crossing his bandy legs.

She mustered a grin. "Cocoa?"

"Felicity!" The goblin looked shocked. "This shirt cost me seven gold flupoons. If I got even a tiny drop on it..."

"Seven! What a rip-off. My mum always buys me stuff in the sale."

"Shush!" He shuddered. "Not the 'S' word."

Felicity rolled her eyes. "You must be the biggest poser in Eternus."

"Yes," he smirked. "Nine years on the trot. Next year I get to keep the trophy and free mollymincer burgers from The Droopy Wand Café.

Felicity had to chuckle. "Good to er, see you."

The goblin promptly fell off the desk. "Who kidnapped the real Felicity?" he blustered, jumping to his feet. "Is she locked in the cellar?"

"The thing is," Felicity persevered, "why do you keep risking your neck for me? First, the night demons, then the Skanky Hags and now -," she shrugged, "- a plane flown by a bunch of terrorists. How did Glumweedy do that, by the way? Send me to the past?"

"He's a very slippery wizard. Smart too and cunning. He enjoys a good fight but only if he wins. By showing you how powerful his magic is, he thinks he can scare you off. Did it work?"

"No." Felicity looked affronted. "I love The Wishing Shelf. There's no way he's getting his chubby hands on it." She wandered over to the sofa. "So the people I met, they did exist?"

The goblin followed her "Possibly, but nobody can help them now. Try to understand, Brady, Glumweedy simply tossed you into a history book, but the final chapters had already been written." He paused. "Did he hurt you?"

She turned and looked at him, her lower lip trembling. "On the ship, a boy drowned. He held my hand, my left, he had tiny fingers. A man, Spink, his name was Spink, he got shot. I held his hand too."

"Forget them."

"HOW!?" She slapped her brow. "THEY ALREADY LIVE IN HERE!"

"Oh, stop bellyaching and show a bit of pluck. I thought it ran in the family."

"You never met any of my family," shot off Felicity.

The goblin grunted and looked to his cowboy boots. Felicity scowled. Or had he?

Look, if Mayor Glumweedy wins, every book in this shop will be slung in a skip." He slumped on the sofa, winching his legs up on the coffee table. "Get a grip, Brady."

Puffing out her cheeks, she hovered over him. "Why do you keep on bothering me?" she challenged him. "There's no gold bar under my bed, no pearls tucked in my hockey socks..."

"Who rattled your cage?" the goblin interrupted her, scratching his dangly ear. "I pop in to say hello and all I get is insulted." He glanced around the shop. "You know if you were a bit nicer, you might get the odd customer."

"You are the odd customer!" she shot back at him.

The goblin chuckled. "Touché!"

Felicity folded her arms and glared down at him, her shoe tapping the wooden floor. "First, get your smelly paws off my coffee table. Second, the shop is deserted because there is a monster hiding in it who enjoys a witch or two for lunch." She snapped her fingers and grinned. "There's a good idea. Why don't you go for a wander, hunt for a good book, GET EATEN!"

A pained look fell on the goblin's chubby face. He clutched theatrically at his chest. "What cruel, cruel words," he scoffed.

Felicity rolled her eyes. "And where are my HobNobs?"

Banks patted his fat tummy. "Why, you got a second packet?"

Just then, Al skipped in the room. He spotted Banks and grinned. "Greetings," bawled the imp, flinging out his hands. "How can I help you today? Do you fancy a book on fishing by magic or a copy of 'Hallowe'en. What to Wear to Scare'? Excellent book."

"No," butted in Felicity, "he needs a copy of 'Get Out of My Shop, You Fat Lazy Oaf'."

The imp nudged her. "I don't think we have that," he whispered. "Who's the author?"

"Al, this is Banks. Remember Banks? Evil, nasty goblin. We hate him."

The imp frowned and looked as if he had just put on a thinking hat. Then he slapped his brow as if trying to waken the memory. "No, nothing there."

The goblin sat up, lifting his feet off the table. "You can get me a mug of bath scum and semolina tea, a sprinkling of bat droppings, whisked up, go easy on the ketchup but lots and lots of slug goo."

The imp's eyes grew wider and wider. Felicity wondered if he had just fallen in love. "Yes sir," he swooned, clasping his hands to his cheeks. "Pop y' feet back up, back in a sec." He saluted and dashed off.

"Cheerful chap," murmured Banks, getting comfortable.

"Oooh, can goblins marry imps?"

"Brady! Really! Green is NOT your colour. Anyway, my eyes only see you."

Felicity doubled over, pretending to throw up. "NEED A PAPER BAG! NEED A PAPER BAG!"

The goblin snapped his fingers. "Here. Stick it on your head. Stop! Stop!" He held up a hand. "There's no need for us to fight every day. Anyway, I can help you catch this monster."

Wrinkling up her brow, Felicity shrugged and checked her jeans pockets.

"What you doing now?" groused the goblin. "Kids! Always fidgeting."

"Looking to see how many flupoons I have." She discovered a nugget and tossed it to Banks.

The goblin bit it.

"Hey!"

"Just checking."

Felicity gritted her teeth. "I have a nasty feeling if you want to help, it is going to cost me."

Tittering, Banks dropped it in a silk pouch and stuffed it in his pocket. "Maybe, Brady," he admitted, "but a grubby gold nugget is not going to cover it."

Smarting, Felicity bawled, "Sofa, up, up, up!" And the insolent goblin tumbled to the floor.

The imp was rolled up in a ball on the sofa, his knees propping up his chin. "Go on," he pleaded. "Just a log and a tiny sliver of coal."

Felicity shook her head adamantly. "If you want a fire we need logs and coal, but to buy logs and coal we need a bucket of gold flupoons, but to get a bucket of gold flupoons we need to sell a book. How many have we sold?" She ended her speech, her fists glued to her hips.

"Is that a no, then?" carped the imp. "But my feet feel like blocks of ice. I think my toes will drop off soon."

"Then drink your ladybird and bumble bee tea. It'll warm you up a bit."

"But how?" demonstrated Al, glaring at her. "It's frozen solid."

"Then pick it up and suck on it!"

They were sitting in The Wishing Shelf but they were soon going to hunt for the monster. Felicity slapped her open palm with a rusty poker she'd found next to the fire. She was planning to bring it with her. The imp had fetched a tiny net on a bamboo cane from the junkroom but she had a feeling the monster would be a tad bigger than a goldfish or a crab. And much bigger teeth too.

She had sent Banks packing. She did not need his help. If only Hickory and Kitta were here but they had left a day ago to go to Lupercus Castle to plan the wedding.

"Felicity," droned Al.

"What!?" She felt like strangling him; he was the biggest wimp in Wimpdom.

"The cup's stuck to my lip."

Clenching her fists, she opened her mouth to bawl at him but then bit her tongue. She was the boss now. It was her job to spur on her staff, not to be a horrible pig like Tantalus had been. She grabbed up the imp's Arctic parker off the back of the sofa. "Pop this on, silly."

Shivering, he did as Felicity instructed, and it did hide his silly t-shirt. On the back in bold, black letters,

THE IMP RIGHTS ACT

1252

And on the front, flashing bubblegum-pink,

CAT FLAPS FOR IMPS

"Come on, then," she chided him, rubbing the top of his head. "Have you got your net? Good boy. Let's go catch a monster."

The cup was still stuck to Al's lower lip. She snatched it off, the imp's yell bouncing off the walls.

Clutching a candle, the poker hanging on the belt of her jeans, Felicity led the way. Soon they were squeezing by tall stacks of books that loomed over them like city skyscrapers.

The imp trudged after her, dragging his feet and the net on the floor. He was snivelling too and kept dabbing his injured lip. Shaking her head, Felicity dug in her pockets and tossed him a hanky. They'd be lucky to creep up on a gang of JCBs, slurping beers and discussing the problems of bulldozing.

Felicity wished the floor did not creak so loudly and the dancing shadows from the candle did not resemble claws and ghostly eyes. Unhappily, not a wisp of sunlight penetrated this far in. Why was it that wizards could do magic, freeze time, even fly on carpets, but they had not invented the light bulb?

"Hello, luvvy."

Felicity jumped, spilling wax on her fingers. But it was only the 'Witch Spotter's' book, perched on a shelf just next to her head.

"Blimey!" she croaked. "I almost peed my pants."

"Almost! I did," muttered Al. He crossed his legs and smiled weakly.

Felicity had to chuckle.

"No, really..." A yellow puddle was slowly forming by his feet.

Stepping away, Felicity wrinkled up her nose. "Yuck!"

"No problem, Boss." Al snapped his fingers. "I know this wonderful charm."

Felicity screwed up her face in disgust. "You know a charm for THAT!?"

But the imp just shrugged. "It happens all the time. I scare very easily, you know."

Shrugging her shoulders, Felicity turned her back on the soggy imp. She looked up at the flapping book. "Anything small and ugly passed this way recently," she nodded at Al, "apart from him?"

"Oooh, yes, my luvvy." A ripple ran down her spine. "But only for the turn of a page. It darts from shelf to shelf like a stray firework."

Felicity chewed on her lip. "About how big are his teeth?" This seemed a prudent question.

The book scratched her spine. "Well, you know how big a wolf's tooth is?"

Felicity nodded. That sounded okay.

"A lot, lot bigger than that."

"Oh."

By her knees, the imp gulped and crossed his legs. "Oh boy," he mumbled.

Felicity heard the trickling of water and she took a bigger step away from him. Gloomily, she looked down at the rusty poker and the goldfish net in the imp's trembling hand. This was not going to work.

Al tugged urgently at her sleeve. "I think I need to pop back."

"Why?" she asked him crossly. "Remember, we have a job to do."

"Why!?" The imp looked at her quizzically. "I need to go to the loo, dummy."

Felicity's face softened. She did not want to listen to him quoting whatever paragraph covered 'Loo Breaks' in the Imp Rights Act of 1252. "Oh, okay. Just be quick."

His hand trembled as he passed the net over to her. Then, he waddled away, his hands fastened to the front of his shorts.

"Oooh, eeeh, aaah," the imp squeaked as he took each step back to the front of the shop. He shuffled by the sofa and there he stopped. Sitting on the floor was a teapot. His teapot. He had lost it a week ago. He recognised the chip on the spout. Oddly, it was sitting in the middle of a big, black 'X'. Al, not being the smartest penny in the pot, wandered over and picked it up.

It only took a split second for the net to fall on him and like a fly in a spider's web, he was trapped.

"FELICITY!" he called, his teeth chattering in fright. "HELP!"

A glittering yellow puddle swelled by his feet.

"Oooh," crooned the 'Witch Spotter's' book, looking distressed and flapping her covers. "Did you hear that?" She clambered up onto the top shelf and scanned the shop. "I can see the monster and – oh no, I think your imp is in a spot of bother."

Dropping the net, Felicity clenched her fists and gritted her teeth. "If only Galibrath had gotten a rottweiler," she muttered, "but no, he gets a poodle."

Like a sword, she clutched the poker in her hand and sprinted back to the front of the shop. Doing an Olympic hurdle over the sofa, she discovered the imp struggling in the net and the monster looming over him, grinding his green beak.

For a long, long moment, it glowered at her and she fervently wished she had listened closer to the imp's 'Peeing Charm'.

To Felicity it looked a lot like a really big duck, not Orville, or Big Bird off Sesame

Street, all feathers and motherly wings, but a hive of craters, dribbling drool and Hitler-crazy eyes.

Then it howled, "Flubby, lubby lub," snapped up the ends of the net in his beak and, dragging the imp with him, he sprinted away.

Chapter 16

Google! Who Needs Google!?

Like a mannequin, Felicity stood in the dark shop and stared forlornly out of the window. She felt tired, her mind crammed full of sinking ships, Spinks' rotten feet and flying terrorists. What a crazy world she lived in. Drops of soft sleepy snow splattered on the glass and the grey tiled roofs of Twice Brewed. To her surprise, the sun was already coming up as if dawn and dusk had been holding hands. One by one, the street lamps blinked off, the milkman clattering by in his electric cart.

She had been the last person to walk in the door to The Wishing Shelf so it was Twice Brewed in England she could see. But if a goblin popped in, or a wizard or a troll, she'd now be seeing old hags tottering by the murky glass.

Soon, the baker up on the bridge would be firing up his ovens and she'd be forced to open the shop, but selling books was the last thing on Felicity's mind. Her imp had been snatched by a monster and now she had to think of a way of rescuing him. If he had not already been garrotted and hung up on a hook. Where was Hickory Crowl when she needed him? Or Kitta, or even Banks? Maybe she would have to accept the goblin's help, after all. She gritted her teeth, her hands balled up and slippery in her jeans pockets.

She glanced about the shop, trying to ignore The Clock by the Door that was ticking in her head like a bomb. Her nose and chin were freezing and the cactus on the coffee table had cheekily put on a scarf and a woolly hat. But she could not be bothered to put a log on the fire. The Wishing Shelf had been empty for days anyhow. She wondered idly if it was only because of the monster or because a girl was now the boss. She shrugged and bent over to do up her lace. What the heck, it was up to her now.

"But what am I going to do?" The words spilt bitterly from her cold lips.

She yelped, hopping to her feet, as the Biro the handyman had given to her jumped up out of her jeans pocket and darted over to the window. She watched, her hand cupping her mouth, as it scribbled on the frosty glass.

Lost your way? In a rut?
Light a candle, read a book.

It flew back over to her and nestled back in her pocket as if it had written a really long essay and badly needed a snooze.

Wow! What a fantastic gift. She must thank him. Buy him a new hammer, perhaps. She scratched her chin, wondering how it worked.

Felicity's brow furrowed, a plan forming in her mind. She needed a book on monsters. If she genned up on it, she could work out how to trap it. But there was only one shelf in the shop where you could find books on evil monsters. She did not want to go back there for it was there that Incantus Gothmog had crushed her legs. But what alternative did she have?

Turning her back on the window, she set off to find the shelf of black books. But no matter how many lefts or how many rights she took, she could not find them. It was as if they were hiding from her, or maybe in a typically magical way, you could only find them if you were not looking for them. But Felicity had a backup plan. She hobbled over to the kitchen to get her scarf and mittens. She would pop to school and jump on a computer. There would be lots of information on monsters on Google.

Suddenly, she felt as if a hook and line were dragging her by the belly button, and in the snap of a finger she was back next to the shelf of black books.

"Wotcha Brady," shrilled a book. "How's the knee?"

The other books on the shelf chuckled.

A second book shuffled up to her and growled. "Fancy a dance? A can-can or a cha

cha cha?" It sniggered. "Oh no, you can't, you being a cripple, an' all."

But Felicity stood her ground. "I have only one word for you all. Bookworm." The black books shuddered and fell silent.

Tilting her head and trying to ignore the odd soft growl, Felicity browsed the titles. 'The Three Ms: Murder and Mass Murder', 'Killing Kittens, A Hobby or a Job?', must show Banks that, 'Monsters. Kill 'em, Trap 'em But Never Marry 'em.' Perfect! She was glad to find a book so quickly. She was beginning to feel a bit sick and she was scared a book might jump off a shelf and chew her nose off.

Gritting her teeth, she grabbed hold of the book on monsters and pulled, but it was as if it was glued to the top of the shelf. That, or the books next to it were hanging on and pulling too. With a bit of jiggling and a mighty yank, it broke free. She stumbled back, her knees hurting as if they were on fire. Gently, she perched on a stool and opened the book.

On page 1 she found a drawing of an anteater eater. It looked a bit like a

Volkswagen camper van but it had one hundred and twenty-seven legs and a curved horn where the windscreen wipers would have been. On page 2, there was an apopossynoceros. She read on, 'This is a very dangerous monster. On the 'Let's-not-invite-it-to-my-birthday-party Richter Scale', it rated five stars. Be warned, the female apopossynoceros has a nasty way of puking over her prey, particularly if she has just had a bowl of spring onion and vegetable soup.' She read about chisel-jawed chompers, humped-back spriggle worms and mollymincers, until she discovered the monster that she had seen. It was called a woolly glumsnapper.

Woolly Glumsnapper
(Laneus contristoictus)

The land of Eternus is full of monsters. They kill and chomp and chew, they hide in caravans and jump out of the shadows. But the glumsnapper is different. It works in a pack and enjoys a good party. It is most happy on a pub crawl, having knocked back twelve jugs of Grogbog beer and a bongeroo worm kebab and chips. When cornered, but for the shubablybub, the glumsnapper can be the most dangerous monster in this book. A cage will not hold it. His hooked beak will rip the mesh to bits as if it were strings of candyfloss. The trick is to trap it in a dark hole, and then just let it be, for a glumsnapper, away from his pack, will slowly wither and crumble to dust.

Felicity stared transfixed at the floor. So she had to dig a hole. Maybe she could borrow one of her dad's shovels. He had two or three in his toolshed. Shutting the book, she stood up and lugged it back over to the shelf, but when she slotted it back on the shelf, the book next to it, 'How to Thwart the Grim Reaper's Reaping', nibbled at her thumb. She skipped back, the book on monsters cartwheeling to the floor. It lay there, growling.

Felicity crouched down to pick it up, but her hand stopped. The book had fallen open and there, glaring up at her, was the very monster that had been haunting her dreams. She looked closer. Oddly, there were only two words scrawled under the picture,

194

HOW TO STOP IT

'Shubablybub Sands,' she read.

Felicity left the book of monsters lying open on the floor and tiptoed away. She glanced over her shoulder. Already, there was no sign of the shelf of black books and she had no idea how to get back there. She felt her body slowly relax. They had really frightened her, goose bumps popping up on her arms and legs, and she hoped never to go back.

But now she had the most difficult job of all to do. She had to hunt for Bartholomew Banks, probably in the Ye Olde Banshee pub, and beg him to help her to catch this woolly glumsnapper.

Felicity sighed dejectedly.

The future of The Wishing Shelf rested in the hands of a wicked goblin; a goblin who enjoyed chopping up kittens and baby hamsters for a hobby. Or was it a job?

Typical!

Only a week to go till the wedding so I had better buy them a gift. Pop to the shops later. I can buy them almost anything in England. They will probably get lots of magic stuff but nobody will think of buying them a toaster. Wizards will not even know what it is.

Problem, there's no electricity in Eternus. I know, I can tell them it's a letter holder.

Going to hunt for Banks soon. I will check the pub. Will probably find him in there chatting up the landlady. Problem is, nobody is coming in the shop so nobody is signing my scroll. I must trap this glumsnapper and tell everybody it is safe to shop here. But I only have a few days left. And I bet Glumweedy is busy getting hundreds of wizards to sign his.

Oddly, this woolly glumsnapper in the shop is not the monster that keeps waking me up. But I spotted it in the book too. They call it a shubablybub. I wonder why it keeps invading my mind every night.

Need a cunning plan!

Still not finished maths work. Miss Stern is going to murder me. Her and the rest of the world.

Chapter 17

Levi Blagoon is not a Pirate

"You know, I am seeing this wonderful boy," Felicity blurted out. She was telling a bit of a porky, but it was only Banks and he had kissed her and she had not yet forgiven him. She puffed out her cheeks. Her very first snog wasted on a warty goblin who had wobbly jelly cheeks and a hundred and seven chins.

Classic!

Banks, who was trudging along next to her, lifted his eyebrows. "Is he...?"

"NO! He's not blind."

The goblin laughed so hard she wondered if he was having an asthma attack. Today he had on a burgundy Polo jumper, a snazzy kilt and a very annoying smirk. Bizarrely, he had on stripy pea-green slippers too. Recovering, he wiped a tear off his cheek. "I was going to ask, is he in your class?"

"Oh." She blushed, her cheeks already pink from walking in the cold. "Er, yes, he is actually. He's in my er, maths class. The top set. He's a trigonometry king."

"Smart chap," observed Banks, then, in a deafening whisper, "What a geek."

He grabbed the sleeve of her jumper and steered her left, past a hag spooning eyeball soup out of a rusty cauldron, a carpet showroom and a shop selling wonky stools. Felicity smiled. She had always wondered why all the stools in The Wishing Shelf were a bit wobbly. She looked up to see a wizard shoot by them on a carpet honking his horn, and she had to step into a shop to let a spotted cow clip-clop by.

She had on the jumper Kitta had given to her for her birthday. On departing the cosy shop, the wool had instantly thickened so she still felt warm. But she had a nasty feeling she now looked a lot like a grizzly bear.

They were in Eternus, in Twice Brewed. Life had returned to the town now Articulus had been destroyed and Gothmog had been killed. Everywhere she looked, imps stood on buckets selling Quill 'n' Scrolls to scurrying wizards and she spotted spindlysloths lazing in The Droopy Wand Café slurping bubbling brews.

A smile lingered on Felicity's lips. She did love it here.

It seemed they were going to see a pal of the goblin's, a chap called Curly Tongs, who was very good at catching monsters, or so Banks reckoned.

"He's very smart. Really good-looking too." Felicity was building up steam now. "All the girls fancy him, even Violet Petally." Violet had green eyes, long legs and her dad had a Ferrari. "He's so tall, you see." To drive home the message, she stared down at the goblin, his shiny head only just reaching her chin. "Very very tall."

"Lovely."

"Yes, he is." She grinned smugly as they marched past a flying bicycle shop. Felicity shuddered, a nasty memory of flying over a spiked wall in Cauldron City, popping into her head.

"Did I tell you he was tall?"

"Yes, you did."

"Excellent." She flashed the goblin a dirty look. She had a feeling he knew she was lying and was enjoying it.

"So, what's he called?"

"Called?!" she spat, rolling her eyes and lifting her nose to the sky. "He's not a chihuahua."

"Glad to hear it. It would never work. Years ago, I dated a chihuahua but we wanted different things. I wanted to snuggle up on the sofa, Frank Sinatra on the radio, a bottle of Grogbog beer in my hand, but she just wanted them little bone-shaped chews."

Felicity sniffed and stalked on ahead.

"Oy! Boy magnet!" Banks shouted after her, his words dancing in mirth. "This is Curly's shop."

She stopped, bent over and gingerly rubbed her aching knee. She was glad they were there. She had left her crutch in the shop and stalking hurt her legs.

Looking over her shoulder, Felicity spotted the goblin ambling over to a shop window. The glass looked really grimy and was covered in a wire mesh. She limped over and stood next to him.

"Charming," she muttered, trying to peer in, but all she could see were stacks and stacks of rusty cages full of feathers.

Over the door, there was a sign,

A dragon on the roof?
A dorfmoron in the shed?
Call Curly Tongs, Monster Slayer,
To shoot him in his bed.

"How very er, sporting of him."

The goblin grinned and nodded. "Monsters disgust Curly and Curly disgusts..."

"Monsters. Yeah, yeah, I get it." Then, "Levi," she blurted out.

"What?"

"He's called Levi." This was the name of the pop singer she had liked when she was younger. She still had a poster of him on her bedroom wall, next to a group shot of Twice

Brewed FC. She had thought of saying Teddy but after the 'hell date' - Lucy had told her the poor boy had had to spend two days in the dentists - she had a feeling a church wedding was not on the cards.

"Levi what?"

"What?"

"Difficult to remember?" A mocking twinkle played in the goblin's eye.

Felicity glared at him in exasperation. "Of course I remember. Bla...goon."

Banks tilted his head. "Bla Goon or Blagoon?"

"Blagoon." This was getting ridiculous.

"So, he's a pirate."

"No."

"Sounds like a pirate."

"HE IS NOT A PIRATE!"

The goblin had the nerve to smile at her as he elbowed open the door.

"Keep up, Brady," he irked her. "Curly is a wonderful chap, just try to ignore his awful jokes."

Seething, she followed him into the murky shop. If only she had asked Fidget Moth or

Professor Dement to help her, but oddly, they had not been in the shop for days.

Felicity pulled a 'yuck' face. Even The Wishing Shelf had not been this dark and dusty and it smelt of a closet full of decomposing rats. The walls were a maze of cracks and spider webs, and the floor was cluttered with crushed beer cans and old bags of fish and chips. Watching where she put her feet, she walked over to a rusty metal table. On it was a cage and in it sat a fluffy hamster.

How adorable. She squeezed a finger through the mesh to pat it.

"Risky, lass. That critter will nip your fingers off." At the back of the shop, a wizard stepped out of the shadows. "That there is a hell hamster."

"Looks to me to be just a hamster." Felicity was feeling a bit cocky. Her granny had a hamster called Elephant and she had always liked it.

The wizard nodded. He looked so old, Felicity wondered if he remembered dinosaurs. "He's a clever chap. He looks so sweet, then he will jump up, scratch your eyes out and feed on your liver."

With a whimper, Felicity yanked her fingers out of the cage. In the last three months, she had been attacked by a river of Cruor fish, a wolf, a gargoyle, even a grief-stricken creepy crawly.

NOW A HAMSTER!

What next? A drooling labrador puppy? A tiny fanged bunny rabbit?

"And be wary of that rabbit over there," the old wizard advised her. "That's no carrot he's gnawing on."

Even for a wizard and a pal of Banks, Curly Tongs looked a little quirky. For a start, he had the biggest nose ever. EVER! Not the size of a brussel sprout but the size of a cabbage addicted to fertilizer. He had gloomy basset hound eyes and super thick specs, and his lips folded over his gums so he looked as if he was sucking on a straw. He had on a torn green jumper and scruffy rumpled shorts, but he had no socks on his feet. To Felicity's disgust, he had his left foot up on a barrel and he was picking his toes.

"Wotcha Curly," roared Banks, ambling over and slapping the old chap on the back. "How's tricks?"

Sniffing, the wizard shrugged. "Got a joke for you, Bartholomew."

The goblin rolled his eyes. "Oooh, goody."

"This wizard thinks he's swallowed a monster..."

"Okay."

"...so he tells a doctor. The doctor says, 'No, no, all in the mind, old chap.'. But the wizard insists he's swallowed a monster."

"Is this a long joke?"

Curly ignored him. "So, the doctor puts him in a deep sleep and opens him up. When the wizard opens his eyes he sees the doctor standing by his bed, holding a big, yellow monster on a chain. 'Who you trying to kid?' says the wizard. 'The monster I swallowed was purple.'."

SILENCE...Even the rabbit stopped gnawing.

"Do y' get it? Do y' get it? Y' see, the wizard's so nutty..."

"Anyway, this here is Felicity Brady." Banks waved her over. "She's seeing a very clever chap called Levi Bla Goon, but he is not a pirate."

Felicity shot the goblin a filthy look. "Blagoon," she seethed. She strutted over to Curly and offered him her hand. "Ignore him, he's a lemon sherbet. Wonderful joke, by the way."

The wizard took it, looking at her cagily, sizing her up. He showed her his chipped teeth and chuckled. "Spot on, missy." He leant over and whispered in her ear, "Most people want to hammer Bartholomew to a pulp and the rest, well, they have yet to meet him."

At that moment, Felicity decided she really liked this Curly Tongs chap.

"So, what can I be doing for you, lass? By the way, fantastic jumper. I thought a dorfmoron had popped in looking for a barber."

Curly's hands felt like sandpaper and he smelt of salt and vinegar crisps. She spotted he had tired panda rings circling his eyes too. "I have a bit of a monster problem," she told him abruptly, letting go of his hand and deciding to ignore the dorfmoron remark.

There did not seem to be a better way of saying it.

"A monster, hey? SMASHING!" The wizard's eyes glinted. "A big un, is he? Sharp claws? Vampire fangs? Stinks of bat dropping?"

Felicity wrinkled up her brow. "No, yes, yes and no idea, but probably."

The wizard's face lit up. "Is it a shubablybub?"

"No."

"Pity, but if you ask me, they will be here soon. A gobble-de-gook, then?"

Felicity shook her head.

"Good. Annoying little critters, nattering on, yap, yap, yap, how to fix a lawnmower, cost of beetroot, how to cook a cockroach crumble..."

"He's a nasty bit of work. A woolly glumsnapper, I think. I only spotted him for a split second."

The wizard's eyes narrowed and he shot a look at the goblin. "No way," he scoffed. "You been hallucinating. A glumsnapper's not been seen in Eternus for over a hundred years."

"But I did see him," Felicity protested, showing the wizard her palms. "And I looked him up in 'Monsters. Kill 'em, Trap 'em But Never Marry 'em'..."

"Excellent book," butted in Banks.

Curly nodded.

"Excellent?! It kept calling me a Numbskull and trying to nibble off my fingers."

"Excellent book," Banks repeated.

Felicity glared at him. "Anyway, it looked just like the drawing, no hands, googly eyes, frog mouth, craters all over his skin..."

"Okay! Okay!" Curly shook his head. "I think I need a drop of Grogbog."

He fumbled for a bottle that stood on a wooden crate in the corner. He took a long swig. Felicity spotted that his hand trembled and half of it spilled on his bogey-green jumper. Oddly, he had a tattoo of a shubablybub on the back of his hand, a dagger stuck in the monster's chest.

"Felicity," he eyed her sternly, "why did the monster's mum knit three socks?"

"Oh, er..." She hated tests.

"Her son had three feet."

She smiled blankly. "Funny."

"Devil to catch, woolly glumsnappers." Curly wiped his chin on his sleeve. "Like a shark in water, so damned fast. Now, I can trap you a dorfmoron, a demon at a push," he flicked a wink at Banks, "and a goblin's a doddle..."

Banks grunted.

"...but a glumsnapper."

"Aw, c'mon Curly," piped up Banks, "remember all them traps you kept inventing? The Mollymincer Net and the Chomper Snare."

The old man shrugged, his face colouring.

Felicity's hand shot up. "Traps? What traps?" she quizzed him. Maybe he could help them, after all.

"Old Curly here was a WANDD agent a century or three ago..."

"Two," butted in the wizard, irritably.

"Anyway, always in his shed, banging and walloping, inventing stuff. Trying to find a way of snaring dragons and not hurting them." The goblin chuckled and slapped the wizard playfully on his right shoulder. "He always was a bit of a softy."

"I'm no softy now," muttered Curly, looking at him grimly. "Not after..."

The grin jumped off Banks' lips. "No," he mumbled. "Now we shoot to kill."

Felicity's brow furrowed. She wondered what had happened.

"Anyway, half of 'em never worked," pointed out Curly, bitterly. "We just ended up with singed bottoms and chewed thumbs, hey Bartholomew?"

The goblin chuckled. "Do you remember old Bert? What a joker, hey? Do you still see him?"

Curly shook his head, sadly. "Hunting a dragon, he fell off a cliff. Hit the ground like a paper bag full of vegetable soup." The wizard looked solemn as if standing by the bed of his dying granny and Banks looked as if he had just swallowed a bad clam.

Felicity cringed. "But Mr Tongs, there is no dragon," she reminded him, "so no singed bums." Feeling desperate, she added. "A woolly glumsnapper's a lot smaller too. Sort of chicken-sized." She snapped her fingers. "Oh, and he took Al, my imp." How had she forgotten that?

Nodding slowly, Curly drummed his fingers on the hell hamster's cage. The hamster hissed and Felicity spotted it had fangs. "Grabbed y' imp, hey? To be brutally frank, he's doomed."

"Oh."

"My shoulder is crooked," he went on, "my left knee is full of Tarantula milk - no idea why - and the verruca on my big toe is the size of a dustbin lid." Felicity took a hasty step back, scared he may show her. He shook his head as if shaking off his bad mood. "But why not? Just like in the old days, hey Bartholomew?"

Rallying up a lame grin, the goblin nodded.

"Sparkly!" The wizard seemed to be half-pickled already and did not spot Banks' sudden lack of gusto. "Shall we celebrate? Hidden in my cellar, in a nest of dust and cobwebs, is the oldest bottle of Grogbog in Twice Brewed." He scuttled over to a back door and lifted up the latch. "LET'S PARTY!" he yelled over his shoulder. "TELL A FEW JOKES! I GOT TWISTER IN THE ATTIC!"

"Just like the old days, hey?" Felicity mimicked Curly's gruff words. She wondered absentmindedly, if he was Scottish.

"I guess so."

Felicity looked at him quizzically. "What's up, moody git?"

"In the old days, when we battled dragons and dorfmorons, Curly had the strength of a troll and the daring of a shubablybub in a cage of imps."

Felicity felt her spirits soar. "So, he's good, at killing monsters?"

The goblin blew out his cheeks and scratched his saggy bottom. "In the old days," he mumbled, sourly, "he drank a lot less."

Met a very odd pal of Banks' yesterday called Curly Tongs. Surprisingly, he is not a barber. In fact, he traps monsters for a living. A bit of a nutbar I think. Drinks a lot too and he thinks he's funny. Told me a terrible joke. I hope he can help catch this woolly glumsnapper.

I wonder why he's called a woolly glumsnapper? He's not even woolly!

Planning to pop to hospital tomorrow, but in Eternus, not England. Funny Bone Surgery they call it. Maybe a spot of magic surgery will fix up my legs. I think I may need to run when we go monster catching. VERY IMPORTANT! Must run faster than Banks. Then he will get killed, not me.

A spindlysloth popped down from the attic and told me Tanglemoth is missing. So is Fidget Moth and Dement. Maybe the glumsnapper grabbed them and chopped them up for stew! Oh, must do maths homework.

Chapter 18

A Grimy Yellow Caravan on Scalpel Way

The sigfingel, hidden in a pyramid of rocks, had told her to go left, left and left, by a lollipop tree, a bonbon bush and a gobstopper fern.

Feeling hungry, Felicity had stopped at all three for a quick look.

"The hospital's on Scalpel Way," it had yelled at her, waggling a finger like a windscreen wiper in her face.

Felicity limped up to a grimy, yellow caravan and rested her knuckles on her hips. She scowled. Scalpel Way seemed to consist of the Gooftwerp J Falafel Library in the form of a tired old barn, a muddy ditch, the crumbling trunk of a fallen tree, a mob of dented dustbins and this 'thing' from the 1970s.

All of a sudden, there was a squelch, like a plunger sucking on a blocked sink. A very old and rotten wooden sign jumped up from the ditch and waddled over to her. Felicity felt in her pocket and discovered a hanky. She rubbed it over the front of the sign and 'Funny Bone urgery' emerged. A dangly bit of pond weed hid the 'S'.

So it must be the caravan after all. Reluctantly, she crept over to the door, past the fallen tree swarming with black ants. The sign scuttled after her, seemingly determined to do a good job. Her feet crunched on the gravel path and the wind rattled the caravan's windows. It really was a disgusting-looking thing. A tangle of nettles hugged the wheels and clumps of moss erupted from the cracks in the walls. She looked sceptically at the bricks wedged under the wheels and the rotten steps.

Felicity had spotted on page 3 in her dad's paper, The Sun, that Verity, 21, from Liverpool, felt that hospital funding was a scandal. In Eternus, it was obviously a big problem too. But maybe it was like the Tardis in Doctor Who. On going in, she'd discover a maze of smelly bedpans and sick people in gaping gowns.

Lifting her fist, she knocked. Smelly bedpans jogged her memory of Banks when he had popped in to see her in hospital. She wondered idly if she'd get to meet Matron Bendalot.

"What is it?" A shout assaulted her ears. "Trying to fry a dragon's egg in here."

Charming.

She swallowed the last of her gobstopper. "I need to see the doctor."

A latch clicked and the top part of the door rocketed open, bouncing off the caravan wall. A wizard in a Twice Brewed FC cap popped up, oval specs perched on his cauliflower hooter. He seemed a bit cross-eyed and his lips were the colour of an old penny.

"Doctor! DOCTOR!" he bawled, gawking at her like a goldfish. "This is not a hospital."

"Oh." She glanced at the sign, now nuzzling her elbow. "I thought it was."

"Well, yes, in a way." Looking abashed, the wizard kicked open the bottom part of the door. He waved her in. "So, what's the problem?"

"I hurt my legs," answered Felicity, gingerly taking a step up.

He barred her way.

"We only do legs on a Monday."

"Today is Monday," Felicity shot back at him. What a muppet.

Chewing his lip, the wizard stepped back. "Clever clogs, hey?" he mumbled. Then, "DOROTHY! GOT A HOBBLER HERE!" He plucked up a dish cloth and shooed the rotten sign away.

Stepping into the caravan, Felicity thought four things. First, why did all the old wizards that she met smell of a week-old bottle of milk lying on the beach on a tropical island? Second, there was no way she was going to let him keep calling her Hobbler. Third, the caravan was not the Tardis, but in fact, just a very cramped caravan and this led her to number four, why was the wizard shouting when Dorothy was sitting only three feet away?

"Wotcha!" Felicity walked over to her, trying not to hobble and gingerly stepping over a jagged crack in the floor. Although the witch had not been able to save Galibrath, she had helped Hickory and he'd survived. Fifty percent, not so bad.

Dorothy smiled up at her. She was sitting on a bench in a corner of the caravan, next to a flimsy-looking table. "Good to see you." She called to the wizard, "Mr Pepper, pop the kettle on."

Kneeling, the old man twisted a knob on a grimy, badly scared gas cooker. "Fetch this, fetch that," Felicity heard him grumble, "a collar and a lead next and a bone to chew on." She wondered idly if he was Al's long lost uncle.

Peering over Mr Pepper's wild 'I just been electrocuted' curls, she spotted two bunk beds nestled next to the wall. The top bed looked to be empty, the sheets scrunched up higgledy-piggledy on the pillow, but the lower bunk had a witch lying in it, her flipper feet drooping off the end.

"Now, Felicity," said Dorothy, "what's up?"

Bunching up next to the witch, Felicity's left knee smacked the leg of the table. She gritted her teeth.

"Not very big, is it," she grumbled, "for a hospital."

Dorothy chuckled. For a witch, she was very pretty. Wavy brown curls, deep green eyes, not even a wart on her bunny rabbit nose. Her long, dangly earrings spun and flashed and a knitted shawl lay over her shoulders like a thick black spider's web.

"A year ago, a chap called Fester Glumweedy got voted Mayor of Twice Brewed. He's a fat melon, spends all the town's cash in The Droopy Wand Café. So the hospital's suffered badly."

Felicity nodded. "He is a fat melon."

"You met him?"

"He's trying to get his greedy hands on The Wishing Shelf."

Dorothy suddenly scowled, peering over Felicity's left shoulder. "Not yet, Mrs Bistow," she bawled. "The swelling must go down first."

Felicity turned to look. The witch who had been lying in the bunk bed was now sitting up, frantically waving a napkin at them. On it she had scribbled,

STARVING! GOT ANY HOT DOGS?

"Can she not talk?" asked Felicity.

"Well, sort of. She can MOO a bit. Got her tongue trapped in a whisk," Felicity cringed, "so I had to cut it off and put in a cow's."

"A COW'S!?"

"Yep. Killed in a car accident. No idea why the cow was driving. Anyway, the cow had a donor card, so we popped her tongue in there."

"MOO!" went the witch.

They looked over. She had crossed off hot dogs and had scribbled,

HUMPED-BACK SPRIGGLE WORMS?

Dorothy squeezed Felicity's hand. "Watch your back, there's devilry dancing in

Glumweedy's blood and he's got a sack full of dirty tricks."

Felicity nodded grimly. She knew only too well.

Then the witch switched track. "Did you get the shubablybub finger I sent to you?"

"Yep." She showed it to her. "It really helps but my knee still hurts a lot. The thing is," she dropped to a whisper, "I plan to go monster hunting in the morning so I need a bit of a 'pick me up'. I may even need to run."

"So you can catch it?"

"God, no!" Felicity looked shocked. "So I can leg it."

Dorothy toyed with the shubablybub finger. "The thing is, Felicity, this finger is very powerful. The magic in it is stronger than any pill or any brew I can mix for you; difficult to find too."

"It is? Why?"

"Shubablybubs cannot be killed. They all live for exactly a hundred and forty-three years. End of story. The end."

"But what if they get sick?"

The witch smiled and handed her back the finger. "They get better."

"What if I stab it?"

"No."

"Chop it up?"

"No"

"Toast it - in a - toaster?"

Shaking her head, Dorothy shot her a big sparkly smile. "No clue what a toaster is, but I'm guessing - no."

Felicity thought for a second. "Okay, but if I shot a shubablybub - in the eye - with a cannon - a foot away, there's no way..."

"They split in half - that's how they multiply. Then there'd be two of the blighters to fight."

Felicity remembered the drawing of the shubablybub in 'Monsters. Kill 'em, Trap 'em but Never Marry 'em'. It had been soooooooooo ugly. She supposed it had to be better than mating.

"Bongeroo worms can do it too," the witch nattered on. "Clever critters, for worms. The only way to kill a shubablybub is not to kill it;

run away, go for a pint. That's the smart thing to do."

"And Shubablybub Sands?" asked Felicity, remembering the book on monsters. Oddly, goose bumps flared up and down her legs.

Dorothy lifted her eyebrows. "The old hourglass legend? How did you know...?" she trailed off, her eyes misting over. "I remember in school, all the kids had to chant this silly riddle." A shadow draped over her shoulders even darker than the spider's web shawl. "The teacher told us, if we worked it out, we might discover the whereabouts of Shubablybub Sands. Why do you ask?"

Felicity fiddled with a red button on her cardigan. She did not want to tell her. "Do you remember the riddle?" she persisted. "Can you tell it to me?"

Scrunching up her brow, Dorothy thought for a second. "Okay, if I can remember it.

"What is a stick when the blood flows cold?
And the anchoring fingers in, er..."

Dorothy frowned, thinking.

"Ferwig, yes Ferwig,
A yesterday sword or a pistol in hand,
Pyramid on pyramid in a parched, arid land,
Or to bolt a Colonel Custard, or to scarper."

Felicity's chin hit her chest. "What!?"

The witch shrugged. "No idea. I never solved it; nobody ever did. Anyway, the Sands has been lost for hundreds of years. I doubt anybody will ever find it."

"So, these monsters," Felicity kept her eyes glued to the dirty floor, "they live - where?"

"In the land of El-Roth, to the north."

Shoving her hands in her pockets, Felicity grunted. She had a feeling the riddle was important. But how? And why? She had a woolly glumsnapper prowling The Wishing Shelf, not a shubablybub. But every night, in the witching hour, they, not the glumsnapper, invaded her mind filling her with fear. But, even odder still, she had been born in the town of Ferwig and so had her Aunty Imelda.

Looking up, she remarked, "And I bet there's no Matron Bendalot working here."

"Matron who?"

Felicity blew up her cheeks and popped them. "Thought not."

Felicity thanked Dorothy and stood up to go, but Mr Pepper blocked her way.

"Bats' milk, dragons' milk or a lump of week-old, curdled goblins' milk?" he quizzed her.

Squeezing by him, Felicity smiled apologetically. "Sorry, got to dash. Bookshop to run."

"But the pot's on." Perched on the hob a pan of water bubbled merrily. The wizard shot Felicity's back a filthy look. "Mangy kid."

Frowning, Felicity halted by the door. "By the way," she called over to the witch, "what exactly is Shubablybub Sands - and what can it do?"

But it was the grumpy old wizard who answered. "A bleeding egg timer, in it, and it will turn invading shubablybubs to bongeroo worms. Switch off the telly, lass, open a book..."

But Felicity had slipped away.

"Relax, Mr Pepper," Dorothy soothed him. "You can drink her cup now."

Whooping and dancing a jig, the wizard bellowed, "A spot of apple and maggot cake too!?"

Dorothy swallowed. "Okay, if we must."

Over on the bed, the witch frantically scribbled on a new napkin and held it up.

ODDLY, I FANCY A TUFT OF GRASS

Chapter 19

"Can I swap my boomerang for a shotgun?"

"Okay chaps, get to your feet, unplug your lugs and spit out your gum." Curly clapped his hands loudly, making Felicity jump. She shook her head in annoyance. If the monster had been sleeping, he'd now be up and about, knocking back a bowl of Weetabix and planning how to butcher them. "Now, do you all remember the three laws of monster catching? Bartholomew?"

"Plonker," muttered the goblin. He clambered to his feet, rubbing his eyes dopily. He was not a morning-goblin, Felicity observed. Banks had slept on a camp bed and Curly on the sofa in the shop, so they could get up and do a bit of early-morning monster hunting.

Curly scratched his head and scowled. "That'll be a 'no' then. Miss Brady?" He turned to her expectantly.

She shrugged. "Sorry, I skived off monster-catching class," she joked.

Banks tittered and burped.

The wizard flung up his hands. "Chaps, really, try to focus..."

Felicity sighed. "Why did he keep calling her a chap? She was not a boy. Yes, she did like jeans and t-shirts and she was not a big fan of Cindy dolls and prams, but she had boobs. She peered down her jumper. Sort of.

"...this is important stuff," rattled on Curly. He lifted up his thick, milk bottle specs and eyed Felicity sternly. "Heed the three secret laws or the glumsnapper will gut you like a..." He frowned and rubbed his chin.

"Cruor fish?" suggested Felicity.

"A hog in a butchers."

"Yuck." She wrinkled up her nose.

Stuffing his hands in his pockets, Curly paced the room. "Right then, law 1: Always sneak up on the monster on a bearing of 127 degrees and keep your speed to a slow plod of thirteen steps per eleven seconds."

Felicity rubbed her brow. "Did you bring a compass and a stopwatch?" she whispered to Banks.

"Law 2: If the monster spots you..."

"Scarper!" murmured the goblin.

Felicity chuckled.

"...do not," he glared at Bartholomew, "scarper, sneeze, cough, belch, hiccup, scratch or sniff." The wizard dug in his pocket and pulled out a silver hipflask. "And finally, law 3: Very important. Always have a gulp of Grogbog beer prior to the hunt." He uncorked it and took a long swig. "Fancy a tiny sip, Felicity? I always say, a drop a day keeps the shubablybubs away."

"Will it, really?"

The wizard's eyes clouded over. "No," he muttered. "Nothing will keep them away."

She shrugged, "Okay, why not?" She was going to be mauled and munched on anyway. She held out her hand but Banks got to the flask first.

"I don't think so," the goblin scolded her, smacking her fingers away. "Much too young." He took a gulp, coughed, spluttered and went purple.

The wizard chuckled. "Got a bit of a kick, hey? Like dynamite."

Corking it, Banks slipped it in his trouser pocket. "Blimey, Curly, what's in it? Carpet polish?" He seemed to have got it up his nose and kept sneezing.

Felicity hushed him. "The monster!"

The wizard scowled, his fists on his hips. "Hey! My flask! Hand it over, cowboy."

The goblin shook his head. "We can all party when the glumsnapper's trussed up in a potato sack."

"But, but..." Curly looked very annoyed.

"I need you sober, old chap." Banks jumped up on a wooden box and gripped the wizard's shoulders. "This is not a game of Hide and Seek."

Curly forced a nod. "Okay," he mumbled. His lips looked dry already. He turned to Felicity. "What do you do with a green monster?"

Felicity's lips formed an 'O'.

"Watch it ripen." The wizard chuckled. The appalling joke seemed to cheer him up considerably. "My best yet, I reckon."

To Felicity, the wizard today looked a lot like a cowboy. He had on long black boots and a lasso hung on the belt of his torn jeans. Maybe, back in his shop he had a donkey to carry his shovels and cans of beans. Bizarrely, he had on a Stetson and what looked like 'Henry the Hoover' strapped on his back.

She glanced over at Banks. She was happy he had taken the flask away from Curly, but there was no way she was going to tell him that. The goblin held a crossbow in his hands. She had wanted that but the wizard, in his wisdom, had handed her a silly boomerang. Did she have on a hat with corks dangling off the rim? Did she have a pet kangaroo?

Why a boomerang, anyway?

They were hardly hunting kangaroos and fluffy koalas. In fact a woolly glumsnapper was not even woolly.

But Felicity had browsed her 'Book of Easy Charms', so she had a trick or two up her sleeve. Anyway, Banks' silly crossbow did not have any arrows in it, so what good was it anyway?

"Miss Brady did a bit of reading," Curly clapped her on the back, "so now we know how to trap the blighter. All we need is a hole." He walked over to the sofa and rolled back the rug lying next to it. Next, he chanted,

"Dig a hole, sheer and deep,
To trap the monster that we seek."

Wide-eyed, Felicity watched the door to the shop swing open and a line of moles in yellow hard hats troop in. She noticed there were seven of them and she had a strong urge to sing, 'Hi ho, hi ho'. They formed a circle by the sofa and began to dig, throwing up tiny hills of wood, dirt and rocks. After ten minutes or so they stopped, saluted Curly and marched off.

Looking delighted, the wizard unrolled the rug, hiding the hole.

"Now we just have to herd the rascal in there, just like a sheep." Grinning, Curly thumped her on the back. "A walk in the park, hey Miss Brady?"

Felicity shot the wizard a long, sceptical look. She remembered the general in the tent had told her that too. But Curly had not seen how fast the glumsnapper could sprint.

'Quicker than a rocket," the 'Witch Spotter's' book had told her.

On top of that, there was no way she was going to fill in that deep hole.

"Mr Tongs, why is it called a woolly glumsnapper? There's no wool on it."

"It sleeps in a woolly blanket."

"Oh." What a very fluffy, puppy-like-thing for a killer monster to do.

"Okay, lass, time for you to do your bit." Startled, Felicity looked up at the wizard. "You need to tell your books what to do."

Felicity nodded and reluctantly looked over to the coffee table. On it, standing up stiff-backed as if they were on parade, were three books. She frowned. Did her dad tell her to salute with the left hand or the right?

"Can you do it?" she whispered to Banks.

The goblin shook his head. "They will be facing a crazed monster. For you," he added, harshly, "so you need to tell them."

Felicity grunted; she hated it when the goblin was right. "As you know," she addressed the books, "there is a woolly glumsnapper roaming The Wishing Shelf. We must trap it or sell the shop to Fester Glumweedy and if he gets it, he will toss all the books in a skip. I'll be fine, but you lot will be in the bin, dripping wet and smeared in baked beans. So I need you three to go and hunt for the monster and if you spot it, to bolt over and tell us."

"But how will we find you, Miss Brady?" peeped up a scrappy-looking book on rug beating. Now, she owned The Wishing Shelf, the books all called her by her last name.

She felt very important.

The 'Witch Spotter's' book chuckled and nudged the smaller book. "No problem, my luvvy, we can just tell a book on a shelf and he can tell the next book and so on and so on till we find them."

Felicity nodded. "Ace idea." She watched as they scuttled off, jumping from shelf to shelf. She hoped they would be okay and not get injured. She sort of felt like a mum to them now.

Following Curly, Felicity set off, the dodgy boomerang clutched in her hand. The goblin sauntered after them, his hands shoved in his pockets. He was still in a bad mood, chuntering on about how he had missed his croissant and glass of Krugs champagne that morning. If he dared to comment on how fat her bum was she would cut up his Yves Saint Laurent shirt.

Yesterday, Felicity had popped to Focus to buy a torch. She had given it to Curly and he had been delighted. Hunting monsters by candlelight was just silly. If only there had been a gun shop in Twice Brewed; she could have bought a really big shotgun – or a bazooker!

KAPOOW! End of problem.

Creeping by the gloomy rows of books, she decided, now that she was the owner of The Wishing Shelf, she should invest in electricity, lamps and radiators. She loved the old shop but she would love it a lot more if it was less dark, less damp and less scary. In her mind, it was difficult to sell any book covered in green moss and smelling of her grandad's wet underpants.

They tiptoed on, turning to the left and to the right, Curly stopping at every corner to sneak a look. Felicity always clenched her fists, expecting him to jump back in horror or to be grabbed by a bony claw. In her mind, she went over and over a charm she had discovered in her book - and she kept the boomerang ready.

Curly held up a hand and they stopped. What now? The wizard flashed the torch, zapping murky corners as if he held a ray gun. Spotting a book waving madly at them on a shelf, they crept over. Felicity hoped it had a message for them from the books they had sent out on patrol.

"The 'Witch Spotter's' book told 'Get Your Kicks, Grasp Magic Tricks', who told 'Who's Who in a Witch's Coven' who told 'Rabbits in

Hats, A History', who told me..." The book inhaled deeply and coughed.

"Yes?" Curly urged it on.

"That the poodle is in the bathtub but the ladle by the tap is badly bent."

They dumbly stood in a circle, digesting this crumb of dodgy intel.

"You definitely heard 'poodle'?" grasped Felicity, clenching her damp fists.

The book scratched his spine. "That's what 'Rabbits in Hats, A History' whispered to me. I think," he added slowly. "Did he say 'poodle' or was it 'noodle'? He's from Newcastle, very difficult to understand a word he's saying. I can pop back and check." Mumbling, he waddled off back along the shelf.

Curly grunted and set off. "Sloppy troops," Felicity heard him mutter, then, "I wish I had my hipflask."

"I must say," chuckled Banks, nudging her in the ribs, "your books are doing a smashing job."

Felicity bit her tongue and followed the wizard.

"It's so important to know that the poodle is in the bathtub," he rambled on, "and not in the shower. I wonder where the yellow duck is."

"Shut up," she whispered back. She wondered if she'd get away with it if she strangled him.

"And now the ladle is all bent and by golly, next to the tap, we can grab that glumsnapper in the flap of a dragon's wings."

"Barf, go jump off a bridge!"

"You know Brady, you must be the most stroppy human I ever met. Always grumbling, griping, grousing and - getting on my wick."

"I'M A TEENAGE GIRL! THAT'S MY JOB!"

"Shush, the monster." He smirked. "Anyway, I was just trying to help."

"Then, stop trying to help me," fumed Felicity, swinging on him, "and actually help me."

"Okay, okay." The goblin held up his hands in mock surrender.

"So, why *do* you keep trying to help me?"

"I enjoy a good lark and a spot of danger, is all." Pushing up his chest, he reminded

Felicity of a peacock showing off her feathers. "The lads in Ye Olde Banshee pub call me Cap'n Poopdeck Banks, the swashbuckling pirate."

Felicity snorted, stuffing her fist in her jaws.

"Okay then," the goblin looked a little upset, "how do you see me?"

"Small and rather annoying."

Banks glared at her. "Oooh, I wonder if the books could tell us if a fly with no wings is called a walk..."

Felicity stomped off.

"...or how they get a zebra to cross at the black and white..."

Abruptly, the goblins flow of annoying words stopped. Felicity relaxed her fists and peeped over her shoulder, just to check he had not stopped to pose in a mirror. But he was nowhere to be seen. Had the woolly glumsnapper grabbed him? On the floor, by a stack of books was the crossbow. Slowly, she picked it up. She had wanted it but not that badly.

Then, she remembered Curly. She had to tell him. WARN HIM!

She twirled on her heels looking for the old wizard, but he had vanished too. Trying to swallow her terror, she tiptoed to the end of the row of books and cautiously peeked around the corner.

"Mr Tongs," she whispered urgently, "this is not the time to play Hide and Seek, remember?"

A hand gripped her shoulder and she yelped.

"Shhh!"

It was Curly. Felicity felt her shoulders droop, the hammering in her chest slowing to a dull throb.

"Look," the wizard urged her. "Can you see him? Over there on the floor, by the dorfmoron-foot umbrella stand?"

Fighting the urge to run howling from the shop, Felicity peered into the gloom. "Yes," she croaked at last, "I think so."

Nervously, she watched the wizard gently press a red button on the side of the 'Hoover' on his back. It hummed to life. He grabbed for a long nozzle and gripped it tightly in his hands.

"What is that thing?" she whispered.

"M-S-U."

"And that is...?"

"A Monster Sucker Upper."

"So it...?"

"Yep, just what it says on the label. Sucks up terrifying monsters."

"Gotta hurt."

"Agony."

"By the way, I think it took Banks," muttered Felicity miserably.

Curly nodded. "There's always a silver lining." He squeezed her hand. "Just joking."

They stood silently, watching the woolly glumsnapper. Felicity had half expected him to be filing his claws, sharpening his fangs or chewing on Banks' left foot, but in fact, he had his legs crossed and a plump book open on his lap.

Maybe it was a recipe book for goblin stew.

From here, he even looked to be smoking a cigar!

"A monster killed my wife," mumbled Curly suddenly. "A shubablybub."

Felicity looked up in horror. "How, er - terrible," she stumbled. She spotted that the tattoo on his hand glimmered red.

"So, I drink, you see, to forget - and I tell the odd dumb joke." Then, so quietly she almost missed it. "But I am not a loser."

"I know that."

Tearing his eyes away from the glumsnapper, he grinned down at her. "What do you get if you cross a goldfish with a dog?"

Felicity lifted her eyebrows. Not the best moment to be telling a joke. "No clue," she mustered.

"Nor do I, but it's wonderful at chasing submarines."

She forced a smile.

Squaring his jaw, Curly yelled, "FOR MY NANCY!" and he charged up to the monster. The glumsnapper jumped up, dropping the book on the floor. Quickly, it backpedaled, trying to flee the flapping wizard.

Felicity soon lost them in the dark. Then, suddenly, a crash rocked the shop, then a yell, then -

WATER SPLASHING!? How bizarre!

Then - nothing!

A judder of horror slithered down her spine, stopped for a second in her bladder and then unlocked her knees. She collapsed to the floor and rolled up in a ball, her chin digging in her chest.

To add to her shock, a book jumped off the shelf over her head and landed nimbly on her left shoulder. "The ketchup is flowing," it whispered excitedly in her ear, "but the jug of butter is still piddling in the rusty kettle."

It scrambled back up on the shelf and sauntered off, no doubt to tell the other books what a wonderful job it was doing.

Felicity's lower lip trembled. No Curly Tongs! No Bartholomew Banks! NO SHOTGUN! Just a shop full of nutty books playing Chinese Whispers.

She was going to be murdered horribly.

Chapter 20

Crossbows and Dodgy Boomerangs

There was a deep growl and the floor creaked menacingly. Wishing she was tucked up in bed, Felicity dragged her eyes from the safety of her cupped palms and looked up. To her horror, the woolly glumsnapper's drooling beak was only a foot away from her nose. She could see every bristle on his chin, every crater on his bulbous cheeks, and oddly, the smell of lemon lingered in her nostrils. The monster shuffled up to her, a drop of green drool splattering on the jeans of her hunched up knees.

"Flubby, lubby, lub," croaked the glumsnapper. The monster's saucer-eyes narrowed as if it expected her to reply.

What to say!?

Felicity decided to play it stupid; she'd always been good at that. "Sorry, what?"

"Flubby, lubby, lub." He sounded a bit annoyed now but Felicity had no idea what he was trying to say.

"Er, lubby, lub, lub," she ventured. "Lub, lub, lubby, lub, lub - lub."

The glumsnapper bared his gums and growled. Oops, too many lubs.

The monster lifted up a leg, grabbed her by the neck and squeezed. Felicity's life flashed in front of her. It only took a split second, which was a bit disconcerting. She felt claws digging in her skin and she grabbed for his duck-like foot, trying to wrench it away. But he was as strong as a dorfmoron.

A rage filled Felicity from her shoes to the tops of her curls and her eyes glowed in anger. She thrust up her chin, the glumsnapper's whiskers scratching the tip of her nose.

Odd that. Maybe he had lost his razor. That, or trying for the Mexican look.

"GET - OUT - OF - MY - SHOP," she wheezed.

For a second, the claws loosened on her neck. The monster seemed to be confused by her sudden display of fury. Then, it howled and squeezed even harder. Felicity felt her tongue swell up and her eyes seemed to be trying to pop out of her skull.

BANG! A book crunched down on the glumsnapper's head. THUMP! With a Tarzan cry, a second book swung off a shelf and kicked the monster squarely on the chin. In a mass of fluttering paper, hundreds of books leapt on the monster and with a holler it jumped back, letting go of Felicity's swollen neck.

"For king and country," yelled a red book, landing on the glumsnapper's leg. It hung there, head-butting the monster's knee.

"What?" shouted a second book, perched on a shelf, about to jump.

"That's what they shout in the films," the red book shouted back, between head-butts.

The other book fluffed up his pages and dived. "For The Wishing Shelf and for Miss Br..." It missed and thumped to the floor.

Felicity cringed. Got to hurt!

She lunged for the crossbow and the boomerang she had dropped and jumped to her feet. At the end of the row of books, she skidded to a halt and turned to look back at the glumsnapper.

"Oy, Titch," she goaded it. "Catch me if you can."

The glumsnapper growled and shot after her, the books cartwheeling to the floor. Right, thought Felicity, boomerang time. She lifted it up and flung it at the bullet of fur, but it hit a shelf, ricocheted off a stool and darted up into the roof.

"Flippin' heck," she muttered. Flapping up her heels, she sprinted away, the glumsnapper in hot pursuit.

Ignoring her throbbing legs, she dashed by a wobbly stack of cookery books, the tip of the crossbow knocking them over. Over a desk she jumped, followed by the dorfmoron-foot umbrella stand, a rusty bin and a supermarket basket. She really had to tidy up.

Under a stepladder she sped. On it, the handyman, busy hammering at a shelf, bawled, "Who's winning?" He did not even stop to drop the hammer on the glumsnapper's head.

Skidding around a corner, her foot hooked on a crumpled rug and she fell to the floor, dropping the crossbow. There was a twanging sound and suddenly a silver arrow was rooted into the desk. But how? She picked up the crossbow in wonder. The arrows must be invisible till they hit whatever they hit. Different! Still on her knees, she lined it up with the corner.

Seconds ticked by. Where was it? Her hands were trembling and her eyes stung. Then, she heard a tiny grunt over her left shoulder. She was reminded of 'Jack and the Beanstalk' her mum had taken her to see last Christmas. The children had kept shouting, 'He's behind you'.

Twisting her body, Felicity jumped to her feet. She pulled the trigger and held it there. Like a monkey, the glumsnapper jumped up on a shelf, the torrent of arrows hitting the legs of stools and spearing the wall.

"Medic," yelled the 'Witch Spotter's' book, an arrow stuck in her spine.

But not a single arrow hit the monster and the crossbow soon clicked empty.

BLAST! HOW HAD HE DODGED A HUNDRED INVISIBLE ARROWS!?

Gritting her teeth, Felicity tossed the bow at the glumsnapper. She had to get back to the front of the shop and find a way of luring it into the trap. It was the only way to stop it. It could sit in the hole and rot for a hundred years for all she cared.

She shot off, skidded left, hurdled the rug and landed on the sofa. She turned to look for the monster but it was already standing in front of her. Two steps and it would be on the rug and fall in the hole.

She spotted Pyjamas, the cat, perched on top of a stool. It looked at the glumsnapper, yawned and began to lick her paws.

Just like her owner!

She shook her fist at the monster. "Come and get me, you coward," she bawled. She flapped her arms and squawked like a chicken.

But the woolly glumsnapper could jump too and with a mighty leap, jumped over the rug and landed on the sofa next to her.

That was a brilliant plan, she thought, reluctantly turning to face it.

"Okay," she yelled. "You asked for it, Buster." And with her heart thumping with the urgency of a death drum, she chanted,

"A wisp of wind now a howling gale,
A tornado of crisp bags and stabbing hail,
Wrap up my enemy and jiggle him around,
Corkscrew his legs, root him in the ground."

The shop door shook and the window rattled, splintering the glass. A howling wind shot down the chimney and pushed open the letter box. Felicity ducked and fell to her knees. The door sprung open, bouncing off the wall and she looked on in horror as a tornado charged into the shop. Books rushed for cover as stools and desks were spun round and around, shattering as they struck the rafters in the roof of the shop. Pyjamas lay under the desk hissing and spitting as a lamp shot by Felicity, just missing the cleft of her chin. In the corner of her eye, she spotted the glumsnapper being lifted off his feet and, like a screw, drilled into the wooden floorboards.

The wind slowly dropped, many of the books jumping up on the sofa to see what had happened. Even Pyjamas slumped over to peer at the snarling glumsnapper. Felicity slumped down on the sofa, cuddling her knees. "WAHOO!" she yelped, "I trapped a monster. There must be wizardry in my fingers after all!"

But the woolly glumsnapper had a very different plan. Grunting, he struggled free, flying up as if he had been shot out of a cannon and showering the shop in splinters of wood and rusty nails. Yelping and screeching, the books scattered and Felicity, cowering on the sofa in shock, grabbed for the closest thing to hand and lobbed it at him, smacking him in the chest.

Sadly, the 'closest thing' happened to be a brown fluffy cat.

"Blast!"

Warily, the monster clambered up on the sofa, his eyes brimming with fury. If only she had been to karate class – or even typhoo...

Whoooosh!

The boomerang shot by her, walloping the glumsnapper squarely on the hooter. The monster's eyes rolled up and Felicity watched in wonder as he staggered to the very edge of the sofa.

He wavered there.

"Sofa, up, up, up!" she bellowed, remembering the handyman's words.

The sofa shuddered and tipped over, the glumsnapper stumbling off and landing on the rug. Felicity, holding on for her life, watched as the rug collapsed and the monster fell, landing with a bone-crunching thud in the hole.

"Different," murmured Felicity, still in shock and her limbs raw with scuffs and cuts.

She looked over at the shattered window and grunted. It had already been fixed three times this month. "The handyman will think I want to marry him," she muttered sourly.

Pyjamas jumped up on the sofa, hissed at her and then limped off in disgust.

"Sorry," she called, but she had a feeling the cat was not going to forgive her so easily.

Two hours later, Felicity was still looking for Curly and Banks. She had sent books to hunt for them too, but the 'Witch Spotter's' book had been left lying on the sofa, a plaster on her spine.

She was being nursed by a book called, 'Stung, Cut and Nipped. Get Better Quick', who had kindly offered to help her.

"Over here," yelled a book, waving at Felicity.

Almost lost in the maze of rooms, she dreaded what she would find. She turned a corner and there they were. But they were not dangling on hooks and they had not been sliced and diced and fed to dragons. Felicity rubbed her eyes and blinked. They were in fact all sitting in a bubbling Jacuzzi, drinking tea.

"Yoo hoo," called Banks, splashing Curly. The wizard chuckled and tossed Felicity a grin.

All the wizards and hags who had been snatched were in there too.

Matilda Lemming.

Professor Dement.

Even Fidget Moth.

"Hi, Felicity," called Al. "Jump in! Do you fancy a cup of lemon and grasshopper tea?"

Chapter 21

A Bag of Stripy Yellow and Green Socks

Why did it always seem to be drizzling in England, pondered Felicity. Particularly on Sunday afternoons. She had on her mum's orange Mackintosh but tiny drops still crept in her ears and splattered her cheeks and frosty hands.

A swirling mist loitered over Twice Brewed and everybody seemed to be in a terrible hurry. Golf umbrellas threatened eyes and speeding cars splashed unwary shoppers. Smokers stood shivering in the porch of The Snooty Pig, trying to look cool but wishing they had never discovered tobacco. All Christopher Columbus' fault anyway. Him and his bloomin' potato.

In the town park, just over the street from the pub, Felicity and Hickory lolled on the swings. The wizard did not often go to England but when Felicity had asked for his help, he had seemed happy to say yes.

"Big step," she mumbled.

"Yep," agreed Hickory, resting his cheek on the rope of the swing.

"A wedding!"

"Yep."

"Kids next."

"Probably."

"A life full of prams and hunting for a nappy and a dummy." She glanced at the wizard. "And that's just for Kitta."

Hickory chuckled. "It is a big step, but she's so wonderful."

Felicity grunted, non-committedly.

"Felicity!"

"What? Okay, Kitta's not – THAT bad, but..."

"But?"

Twisting on her swing, Felicity looked at him. "In a nutshell, she's bossy and she thinks she's IT! She has big feet too."

Hickory rolled her eyes. "The size of my wife-to-be's feet is not really that important to me..."

"Yeah, but, cost of boots and all that."

"Felicity."

"Or maybe, she's put a spell on you," she suggested earnestly, remembering her week-old theory.

"FELICITY!"

"Just saying." She twisted on her swing trying to get dizzy.

"So, do you still think Glumweedy's going to win? Did lots of wizard's sign his scroll?"

She nodded miserably, shutting her eyes. She had only had The Wishing Shelf for two weeks and tomorrow, the day of the wedding, was her last day. "Been sort of busy trying to catch a woolly glumsnapper, so my scroll is a bit - desert-like."

She stopped twisting.

"Sorry." Hickory leant over and squeezed her shoulder. "I wish I had been there to help, but I had to visit my, er - Uncle Billy."

Oddly, she had a horrible feeling he had just told her a gigantic porky.

"Forget it." She ducked under the tangled rope and stood up, letting the swing twist crazily. "The Wishing Shelf is my job, my responsibility."

Nodding, Hickory got to his feet too. "Maybe a dashing knight will gallop up and whisk you off to his castle in the hills."

"Maybe." She grinned. "But only if his horse is a shiny Ferrari and the castle has a Jacuzzi and a gym."

The wizard smiled too and offered her his hand. "Shall we?"

They sloshed over the zebra crossing to the square. In her hands she clutched a big bag of stripy yellow and green socks. Galibrath had given them to her last Christmas but she had never worn them. They were still wrapped in plastic, 'Size-5' labels sewn in the heels.

They trudged by a wooden bench that had been donated by a Mrs Watson in 1983. 'In Memory of Donald' had been etched on a bronze plaque.

A kid had thoughtfully scribbled 'Duck' and 'That's All Folks' next to it in black pen.

Looking lonely, a stone obelisk stood in the middle of the square. They trudged over to it and stopped. Felicity scanned the list of names carved on the front.

WE WILL REMEMBER THEM
Corporal Steven Cook
Private Jacob Dawkins
Major Robert Cecil Frost

The list went on.

Sadly, she had no idea of Spink's proper name. Anyway, he had been from a different regiment, from a different town. But no matter, Felicity remembered him and his poor, rotten feet.

Kneeling and soaking the knees of her jeans, she placed the bag of socks in front of the stone.

"I only knew you for a day," she whispered, "and there is probably nobody left to remember you now. But I do. I think you were a hero. Here's the bag of socks I promised, to keep your feet warm."

Felicity stood up and turned to go home, not all the water on her cheeks falling from the sky.

"Did they even exist? Spink? Jacob? All of them? Or did Glumweedy just..." she lost her words to a sob.

"Oh, Felicity." Grabbing her, the wizard hugged her to him. She hugged him back and there was no way she was going to let go.

"Will you be my best man?" he mumbled in her ear.

She nodded. "Okay."

He smiled and kissed her cheek.

Tomorrow is the wedding. Everybody will be there, even Curly and Banks. I think my speech is okay and I had a bit of help.

No sign of Glumweedy yet. I guess he will show up soon to toss all the old books in the skip. I need to chat to them all, tell them what happened. Maybe I can even stack a few of them in dad's old toolshed. I can keep the 'Witch Spotter's' book on my shelf in my bedroom. Must pop up to the attic and tell the spindlysloths too. No way they will all fit in the shed.

Had a long chat to Hickory yesterday. He asked me to be nicer to Kitta. I think I will. Maybe Banks is right. Maybe Hickory is a TINY bit too old for me. But not planning to alter my speech, so may upset Kitta anyway. Oh well, will start being nice to her next week.

I guess I need to pop and see Galibrath. He will be so angry I lost The Wishing Shelf. Tantalus will probably be up there too. I bet the nasty git will try and strangle me.

Why is life so complicated?

Tomorrow I say goodbye to Hickory.

Tomorrow I say goodbye to my bookshop.

Why is life so ghastly?

Finished maths work! HURRAY!

Chapter 22

Drooling Party Crashers

Relaxing back on the bench and crossing her legs, Felicity stared glumly at her shiny red stilettos. Appalling was just too charitable a word. And on top of that she had blisters the size of plums on her heel and big toe. In a gigantic effort to look girlie, she had even splashed out on a frilly velvet dress and a glittery handbag off a dodgy market stall. Annoyingly, the silver fur covering it kept catching on her watchstrap so it now looked like a sick cat.

Anyway, she was glad the dress hid the scars on her knees and she did feel a lot taller in the heels, even if she did feel very wobbly in them. So wobbly, Kitta had handed her a glass of water and had told her sternly to sober up.

Fidget Moth, the cheeky gnome, on spotting her in the crowd, had bellowed, "So, she's not a boy?"

Felicity chewed on her lip. No free book tokens for him.

She and hundreds of other guests were in the courtyard of Lupercus Castle, overlooking Twice Brewed. The grey fort had been dressed in fluttering banners and yards and yards of silver ribbon. Even the cannons looked pretty, bells hanging off the barrels and flowers stuffed in the spokes of the wheels. Agreeably, the sun had been invited too and seemed all too happy to smile down on the chattering crowd.

There were wizards, spindlysloths and hags, lots of imps and a gnome or two, perched on pillows so they could see. She spotted Tanglemoth two rows back and waved.

Oddly, the sky was full of birds; not just a few, but hundreds and hundreds of them and they all seemed to be flying south. Where were they off to, she wondered. Usually birds flew south in autumn, not in spring. Well, they did in England anyway.

Wiggly Woo, the band of bongeroo worms the groom had hired, started to strum and bash on the drums. They looked very odd, thought Felicity, like a gang of big curly 'S's with shiny yellow skin, top hats and eyeballs on springs. So this was what the legendary Sands turned the Shubablybubs into.

Al, who was bunched up on the bench next to Felicity, nudged her in the ribs. "Here struts the witch," he chanted in her ear, "she can be a bit of a ..."

"Shush." She slapped his knee. He had on green shorts, a scarf and a freshly ironed t-shirt. It read,

NEVER GO TO BED ANGRY,
STAY UP AND FIGHT

"Remember, any silly tricks or pranks and the imp flap will be nailed up."

Felicity had finally surrendered and allowed a flap to be fitted to the door. Handily, that very day, Dement had decided to be a carpenter. Quicker than the handyman, anyway.

Hickory tapped her on the shoulder. "Follow me," he whispered.

She stood up. In her hand, she clutched her speech. But that was for later. Now, she had to walk to the front, not trip over, find the ring, hand it over and, the most difficult bit of all, look happy.

But Felicity being Felicity, trampled on the hem of her dress, pitched over and landed on, to her horror, Bartholomew Banks' lap.

He grinned at her. "Felicity, not now, but if you want to dance later..."

She jumped to her feet, called him a, 'Sleezy git' and, thankful he had not snogged her, limped after Hickory.

"Wonderful start," she muttered.

"...so, the vicar jumped up and tossed her back her bumblebee socks!"

The crowd howled with laughter.

Kitta's dad grinned. "Now, may I hand you

over to the best man."

Felicity stood up.

"Thanks, er, Kitta's dad." She hiccupped, a nervy thing she always did. "When Hickory asked me to be his best man, I did try to tell him I was actually a girl. To help, he did a whisker-growing charm on me but Kitta stopped him only half way, so I now have very bushy eyebrows and a curl over a foot long on my left buttock."

They all laughed.

"I was chosen to be the best man because Hickory did not trust any of his old pals not to bring up sheep."

A second bigger laugh. Even Bagel, Hickory's dog, seemed to be enjoying her speech; he was yapping by the wizard's feet.

"When I asked Hickory why he was marrying Kitta, he told me, 'For love'. When I asked Kitta, she suggested a new coffee pot would be nice."

Kitta's dad guffawed, choking on his raspberry muffin, but his daughter did not seem so amused.

Excellent news.

"I loved the ring Hickory got for Kitta. Diamonds, emeralds too, I think. But never forget the three other rings, suffering, torturing and enduring.

"I'm only fifteen so I'm probably not the best person to tell a new man and wife how to be happy. But I do suggest Hickory learn two words and never forget them...'Yes, darling'. No, no, just joking. In truth, I wish you years of laughter, years of joy and lots and lots of baby wizards and hags."

She lifted up her glass. "To Hickory and Kitta, happy ever after."

Everybody cheered and clapped. Felicity blushed, bowed awkwardly and collapsed back onto her bench. Her speech had been a success. Thanks to Curly, who had given her all the jokes.

She snuck a look at Hickory. He was cheering too, his hand over Kitta's on the table.

Kitta's dad stood up, knocking over his wine glass. He seemed to be a bit drunk. "The Wedding Song," he declared loudly.

So, to the tune of 'This old man, he played

two..." everybody began to sing:

"A witch and her groom, A magic silver spoon,
A coffee pot, a book of spells, a poppodil or two,
Kiss, kiss, dragon's hiss, a tube of super glue,
A trip to sunny Vegas or a tent in Mangbaloo."

Felicity had no idea of the words so she sang, 'banana, banana, banana'.

"Chopped chomper eggs, Grogbog kegs,
Smoked Cruor fish on a bed of gargoyle legs,
Slurp, slurp, dragon's burp, jump up and cheer,"

Everybody grabbed a glass of Grogbog and stood up.

"Baby's yell, nappy's smell, twins in a year."

"I must say, Mr. Glumweedy, Sir," bellowed Ratchet, "I'm awfully surprised we got invited to this wedding. I never even met this Crowl-chap - or the witch."

Glumweedy, looking smart in a sparkling crimson-red tuxedo, scowled. "I'm surprised too - that they invited you."

The two wizards were sitting on a flying carpet - a very posh flying carpet: twin-turbo with fluffy dice; it had cost Glumweedy a hundred gold flupoons, well, not Glumweedy, but the coffers of Twice Brewed. The money had supposed to go to Doof Bumpplumptwerp's School for the Gifted Gargoyle for a new gym.

"But I'm the mayor," prattled on the podgy wizard. "A very important and, might I say, influential man in this town. I'm forever being invited to funerals and weddings. I prefer the funerals; the grub's much better. I usually only stay a half hour, scoff all the food, say a few words, y' know the sort of thing: We will miss Bob terribly but he had a good life, blah, blah, blah, or if it's a funeral - HA!" He chortled at his own poor joke. "In my speech today, I think I will tell everybody I'm the new owner of The Wishing Shelf."

"But, Sir," butted in Ratchet, "maybe this is a trap. Maybe..."

"Claptrap! Remember, I do the thinking, you do - whatever I tell you to do. Y' got the scroll, yes?"

Looking miffed, Ratchet nodded. "In my pocket," he mumbled huffily.

"Excellent! The Brady-girl's been so busy chasing the glumsnapper, probably the only person who's signed her scroll is her. A fantastic plan! Who thought of it? Oh, yes! ME!" He tittered. "I must admit, I had a very difficult time winning over the town folk myself. Many of 'em seemed to think The Wishing Shelf was a pretty good bookshop. Odd! But, no matter, they were too scared to go in there and sign her scroll, anyway."

They flew over the bustling town of Twice Brewed and up the hill to Lupercus Castle.

"Who own the old castle now?" Glumweedy quizzed the second wizard.

"Jasper Pottywalrus. Busy chap. He's set up a hotel in it. I got a letter from him only yesterday; he's planning to put a pool in the courtyard so he wants a permit." Ratchet blew on his hands, his eyes greedy. "A rich man, old Jasper, but we shall see just how rich he is."

Glumweedy piloted the carpet lower, stopping fifty-odd yards down the hill from the castle, just by Clodcorn Windmill. "Off y' get, Ratchet."

"But, but - I shall be so late," stuttered the wizard, looking to his watch. "The wedding started two hours ago."

"Oh, stop sniveling, Ratchet. I'm the mayor, remember? Not the hired-help." Glumweedy shoved the wizard unceremoniously off his carpet. "There's no way I - me - a wizard with so much power can be seen with a lowly worm from The Planning Department. Anyway," he called, lifting off, "look at it this way: just think how important you will look arriving even later than me."

After a dinner of chisel-jawed chomper eggs and humped-back spriggle worms (Felicity gnawed on a carrot), there was dancing. The

Wiggly Woos really got things going and soon half of the guests were stepping the cha cha or spinning a tango.

Felicity was chatting to Curly Tongs - who seemed a bit perturbed by all the birds fleeing south - when Hickory wandered over. "Fancy a dance?"

"O - Okay," she stuttered, nodding stupidly like a plastic dog in the back window of a car.

The wizard took her hand and led her over to the dance floor. "Chat to you later," she called to Curly, but he did not even seem to see her go, his eyes fixed on the sky.

"You look very happy," ventured Felicity.

"I am."

"I guess you will be living over by Cauldron's Rim, in Kitta's old cottage."

"No. In my house in Twice Brewed, so you can pop in every day to visit us."

"Cool." Felicity meant it. She just hoped the barking bins were no longer parked by his gate.

"By the way, thanks for the letter holder."

She stifled a grin. "No problem."

"Y' know, my life changed the day you

hammered on my door."

"We had to hammer, we broke the knocker," Felicity remembered.

The wizard grinned. "I just knew it was you."

She rested her cheek on his chest. "Thanks," she murmured sleepily.

"For what?"

She lifted her eyes to his. "For being my hero."

Hickory stopped dancing and gently took her chin in his hand. "Can you do me the smallest of small favours?"

Felicity nodded enthusiastically. She'd rip off her own foot for this man. "Anything," she gasped.

"Can you try - just try, to be a little nicer to Kitta. Now, I know she can be difficult too but..."

Felicity snorted. She'd rather rip off her own foot.

"...but she's my wife now and will be forever, and you..."

"Yes?"

"My baby sister."

Felicity summoned up a smile. "Okay."

Hickory hugged her. "Say!" He took hold of her shoulders. "Did you meet my son, Dexter?"

"SON!?" Felicity's jaw slumped. "When did you get a son? How did you get a son? I mean, I know how, but, but, but…"

He put his fingers to his lips, shushing her. "Remember in England, I told you I visited my Uncle Billy?" He shrugged. "Sorry, a tiny porky on my part. I actually went to see Dexter."

Hickory took her hand and led her over to a pyramid of cannon balls. Next to it a boy stood chatting to Kitta.

"Dexter, this here is Felicity, my best man."

The boy did not look round, his eyes staying fixed on the band of worms. "Hi," he mumbled.

"Hello." She offered him her hand. He took it and shook it limply but he still did not look at her. Charming. Not his dad, then.

Hickory looked embarrassed and swigged his beer.

Felicity squared her shoulders. "So, do you

enjoy charm school? Must be difficult getting only F minus."

Dexter reluctantly shifted his eyes to Felicity. They were green, just like his dad's and a mass of straw-blond curls crowned his head. Felicity's fingers itched to yank them out.

"Is it true," he drawled, "that you have the magic powers of a wet doyley?"

Felicity scowled. He'd been talking to Banks. "I may not be top in magic, but I am top in manners. Can I give you a lesson?"

But a shout of, "Where is she?!" interrupted the boy's reply. The shout was chased by the hefty body of Fester Glumweedy and on his heels a jumpy-looking Mr Ratchet. The wizard bulldozed his way up to Felicity and shoved a thick, rolled-up scroll in her hands. "Two hundred and two. I win!"

With a helping hand from Ratchet, he clambered up on the pyramid of cannon balls. "Over here! Over here!" he bellowed, wobbling a little and waving over the bemused guests. "Can everybody see me? Excellent! Now, you all know me, the mayor of Twice

Brewed and the owner of Stuff Y' Pets. But now I'm also the new owner of The Wishing Shelf shop. Over the next few weeks, I will be tossing all them old books in a skip and putting a second, bigger Stuff Y' Pets shop in there.

"I know many of you pop in The Wishing Shelf just to go to the different magical lands. No problem! Keep popping in. There may be just a tiny, tiny payment now, just to cover costs - you know, upkeep of the door, oiling the hinge, et cetera, et cetera, so forth and so forth." He stuck his hands on his hips as if waiting for everybody to clap. Then he spotted Kitta and smiled. "Hello there, pretty lady, I do a fantastic tango. Fancy a bop?"

The witch rolled her eyes. "You must be joking, Pond Scum."

"Okay, see you later, then." Struggling off the hill of cannon balls, he glared back at Felicity. "I told you nobody can stop me. The Wishing Shelf now belongs to me, girl. Hand over the keys." Bagel, by Hickory's feet, growled. "And keep that nasty dog away from me."

Felicity gulped. She had only managed to get twenty-seven, and most of them had been from the old wizards she had met in Ye Olde Banshee pub. Al had collected a hundred and fifty but had spilt eyeball tea on the scroll. Typical!

But Kitta had not finished with Glumweedy yet. She squeezed Hickory's shoulder. "Darling, how many guests did we invite?"

"Two hundred and two."

"And did they all sign Felicity's scroll?"

Her new husband clicked his fingers and Al skipped over. "Here it is! Here it is!" he chirruped. The imp handed him a scroll, seemingly keen to make up for the disasterous tea spill. "All the guests discussed it over the champagne and they decided Felicity was doing a fantastic job."

Smiling, the wizard unrolled it. "All but two of them, anyway. Oddly, Mr. Glumweedy and Mr. Ratchet here did not sign."

Kitta chuckled, looking coy. "So, we think, two hundred and - Felicity, how many?"

She looked to her shoes, the word slowly

forming on her lips. "Twenty-seven," she mumbled.

"So, that's two hundred and twenty-seven wizards and hags that signed it."

"Not just wizards and hags," butted in Al. "Imps too and spindlysloths."

Kitta tossed it to a harassed-looking Mr Ratchet who took it meekly and slowly started to count.

Hickory hugged Kitta. "My wife is a very clever witch," he declared.

Everybody clapped but for Glumweedy who stomped his foot, yanked frantically on his walrus moustache and thumped Ratchet in the eye. To put it mildly, he seemed to be a bit ticked off.

"I told you nobody can stop me," Felicity mimicked Glumweedy's words. "Well, here's a news flash for you: WE JUST DID!"

Scowling and gnashing his teeth, the wizard stomped over to the buffet and began to stuff his chops with chisel-jawed chomper eggs.

Oddly, crazily, Felicity felt amazingly happy but terribly sad too. Yes, she had won The Wishing Shelf: the door to all the enchanted lands was safe and nobody was going to be tossing the books in a skip, but Hickory was now off the market - for good.

She slipped away and wandered over to the fort wall. Dodging tipsy imps, she slowly climbed the steps up to the battlement. Her left knee still ached and her high heels kept catching in the cracks in the stone, but the shubablybub finger in her bag seemed to be doing the trick. When she had it with her, her knee hurt a lot less anyway.

Resting her shoulder on the wall, she looked back at the party. Nutsy, the pirate, was glugging champagne, but thankfully he still had his pants on. Hickory and Kitta were dancing and Al was sitting next to the woolly glumsnapper, enjoying a cuppa. It had turned out that the monster had not really wanted to hurt anybody but had just been lonely. So, egged on by Glumweedy, he had kidnapped her customers and had forced them to enjoy Jacuzzis, cups of tea and jam donuts. Al, on being rescued, had been very upset and had declared the glumsnapper to be his 'best, best pal'. The long and short of it, the monster was now a member of The Wishing Shelf staff. Felicity sighed. She had lost Hickory but she did have the shop (with a hole in the floor which still needed to be filled in) and a ball of fuzz with fangs and claws to help her.

"I think Kitta looks wonderful. A daffodil-yellow dress. Perfect."

Felicity's head twisted so fast she cricked her neck. There, just next to her, looking a bit like a foggy statue, was a ghost. The ghost of...

"Galibrath?"

"In the flesh," he flashed her a grin, "sort of. No, no, don't try to hug me. I am, after all, a ghost, so you'll probably miss and topple off the wall."

"Oh," she pulled up sharply, "alright, then." She could see he was looking glassy-eyed at Kitta. A century or so ago, they had been madly in love. "You okay?" she ventured uneasily. It was so difficult to talk to grownups, even if they were ghosts.

"Hickory Crowl's a good wizard. Bit of a trickster but honest..."

"You think?" scoffed Felicity.

Galibrath chuckled. "He is now, anyway.

He can watch over her. Keep her safe."

Felicity wished fervently he'd watch over her. Briskly, she turned away. She did not want the wizard to see it in her eyes.

"Listen to me, my girl, jealousy is a terrible thing. It can blacken - everything. It destroyed Tantalus and I'd hate to see it destroy you too."

She mustered a tiny nod. She watched Nutsy dance a jig, frightened to look to Galibrath lest she burst into tears.

"So, you stopped that Glumweedy-fellow?" The wizard shuddered. "Creepy chap."

"Yep. But I had a bit of help." She was trying to be humble.

"Help is a good thing. Now the folk of Twice Brewed know how corrupt and greedy he is, his mayor days will soon be over."

The wizard popped his cheeks. Confused, Felicity turned to look at him. He seemed to be a little distracted and kept glancing over the castle wall. Had he ordered a taxi, she wondered.

"My brother Tantalus says hi, by the way. He wondered if it was a bit of a shock that he left you The Wishing Shelf in his will."

"A bit of a shock!? A BIT OF A SHOCK!? I almost choked on a HobNob."

Galibrath stifled a grin. "I shall let it slip when we next play poker. Rufaro plays too but Tantalus tends to cheat a smidge."

Felicity rolled her eyes and grunted. "Shock! Horror! Why did he do it, anyway? To Tantalus, I fell in the category of," she thought for a moment then snapped her fingers, "PUCKERED CAT'S BUM!"

"He had a very empty life," muttered the wizard simply. "But for Goober, he scared everybody away."

Felicity digested this bit of news. "So, it had to be me or..."

"A puffdolt, yes. Not big lovers of books, puffdolts."

She nodded. "I bet."

"How's the knee?"

"Tip top," she wriggled her toes to show him, "and now I'm all better, I have lots of exciting plans for The Wishing Shelf."

He looked at her sadly. "Good, but you may need to put them on hold for a bit."

"Why?"

The ghostly wizard looked past her, his eyes clouding over. Then he sort of rippled. A ghostly way of shuddering, Felicity guessed. "I think all them monsters over there may keep you a bit busy."

Twisting her head, she looked over the wall to the valley and the town of Twice Brewed. She rubbed her eyes and blinked. The wood on the far hill looked to be moving, but it was not a wood full of trees but a mob of screeching monsters. The very monsters she had seen in the book in The Wishing Shelf, the very monsters who always filled her nights: Shubablybubs!

Felicity gulped. There was no way Kitta had invited all of them to the wedding.

She looked back over to the wizard but he was nowhere to be seen.

Kicking off her heels, she dashed over to the steps. She had to warn Hickory. He would know what to do. She jumped the last three steps and pushed her way into the crowd. She could see Hickory but he was encircled by wizards and hags all wishing him and Kitta good luck.

"Felicity, why the hurry?" A tipsy Fidget Moth grabbed the hem of her dress.

She shook him off. "Not now," she spat.

On reaching the wizard, she grabbed him by the sleeve. "Hickory, Kitta," she gasped, "there's..." She jumped to the sound of splintering wood. The fort gate flew open and an avalanche of terrifying monsters poured in.

"SCARPER!" bellowed Hickory, shoving Felicity away.

The wizard's hand flew to his belt but today, of all days, he had left his trusty golf club on his bed.

Shouts and yells of terror filled the castle. Many of the wizards turned to battle the tidal wave of monsters, conjuring up swords and hatchets and soon many of the shubablybubs fell to the floor, cut and bleeding.

Then, a very odd and worrying thing happened.

The injured monsters' cuts healed and the bleeding stopped. Splitting in two, they jumped up to carry on the fight.

Two of the shubablybubs clumped over and

grabbed hold of Kitta. She screeched, kicking one of the monsters hard on the knee. Hickory, who had hold of her hand, held on doggedly, but they were just too strong for him and ripped her from his grasp. With a cry of anger, the wizard battered his fist on the monsters' chests. By his feet, Bagel growled, chewing on a shubablybub's leg.

Rooted to the spot, Felicity watched the shubablybubs in horror. Wherever she looked, the baying monsters were battling wizards and stomping on imps.

They were disgusting; their skin all burnt and crusty brown, peeling off in long, loopy curls. Big yellow eyeballs like gigantic zits hovered over pulped-tomato snouts, and crocodile teeth erupted from car-crusher sized jaws. They clutched curved swords in skeletal paws, hoofs clip-clopping menacingly on the cobbled yard. Felicity gulped. They reminded her of donkeys crossed with chihuahuas, perhaps with a drop of rhino and a pinch of yellow, rusty skip thrown in.

"STOP! STOP!" bellowed Glumweedy, trying to climb back up on the pyramid of cannon balls. "I'm a very important wizard..." but his words were halted by a slashing sword.

A drooling shubablybub lumbered by Felicity. It stopped and glared at her. Hastily, she backpedaled but all too soon her bum met the fort wall. She was trapped. The monster plodded up to her and grabbed her by the curls, lifting her off her kicking feet. Her eyes were filled with fangs and her nostrils, the rank stench of rotting chicken.

"Let me go!" she hollered, "YOU CREEP!" She kicked it hard in the chest and yelped in agony. It was like kicking a lump of rock.

Then, a very funny thing happened, even for Felicity Brady. The shubablybub sniffed her, lowered her gently to the floor, bowed and bumbled off.

Did she smell of rotten fish?

No boy was ever going to snog her if she whiffed of mackerel.

Suddenly, Felicity felt sharp fingers digging in her shoulder. She spun on her heels, her hands shooting up to protect her eyes. But, thankfully, it was only Dexter.

He shook her roughly. "Grab my hand," he

bellowed. "NOW!"

Felicity gazed up at him dumbly, her mind frozen, her feet rooted in the cobbled floor. She could see her own terror reflected in his cat-green eyes.

Grabbing the sleeve of her dress, he dragged her over to a beer barrel resting next to the fort's wall. They cowered there.

"You know, it really was my job to be the best man. I am his son."

Felicity gawped at him. "What!? Is this the best time?" So that's why he had been so difficult to talk to.

He shrugged and whispered grimly, "So, who invited the creepy monsters?"

Slowly, Felicity shook her head, her eyes fixed on Fidget Moth. With a dagger jammed in his jaws, the plucky gnome had clambered up on the barrel of a cannon. Her chin hit her chest as he jumped on a shubablybub's back, trying to stab it in the neck.

Dexter nudged her urgently in the ribs. "Y' ready, Felicity?"

"To do what?" Her eyes met his and for a split second she felt strong and ready to brawl even a shubablybub.

He flipped her a wink. "To scarper," he pulled her to her feet. "Like a chicken."

"A chicken?!"

"Yep, who knocks on the door only to find she's been invited to a fox's birthday party."

Follow Felicity Brady on her final exciting adventure in CROWL'S CREEPERS

Felicity Brady
and the
Wizard's Bookshop

Billy Bob Buttons

book 1
GALIBRATH'S WILL

Felicity Brady
and the
Wizard's Bookshop

Billy Bob Buttons

book 2

ARTICULUS QUEST